USA TODAY BESTSELLING AUTHOR

RITA HERRON

SAFE IN HIS ARMS

MANHUNT 1 SERIES

Beachside Reads
Norcross, GA 30092

Cover Design: Jeffery Olsen
Cover Photo: The Illustrated Romance, https://illustratedromance.com
Print Design: Dayna Linton, Day Agency
eBook Interior Design: Dayna Linton, Day Agency

ISBN: 978-1-949178-00-5 (Paperbook)
ISBN: 978-1-949178-01-2 (eBook)

Third Edition: 2018

10 9 8 7 6 5 4 3

Printed in the USA

To Dayna Linton—friend, assistant—and lifesaver!

SAFE IN HIS ARMS

PROLOGUE

No one will ever love you like I do.

The first time Geoffrey Jones whispered those words to Mia Matthews she'd thought it was romantic. That she'd never grown tired of his doting affection.

Then it had become obsessive. Smothering.

Threatening.

Terrifying.

She had to get away from him. In fact, she'd been planning her escape for months. Ever since the last time he'd vented his temper on her and sent her to the ER.

He reached over in the bed and spooned her, sliding one hand over her breast to squeeze it. She drew a deep breath as if she was asleep, hoping he wouldn't push for more this morning.

A second later, he whispered in her ear. "You know I love you, Mia. I wish we had time for another round, but I have a breakfast meeting."

Thank God. She was still sore from his *lovemaking* the night before.

Pretending to be the dutiful wife, she rolled over and gave him a kiss. "Have a nice day."

He framed her face in his hands, gentle, almost like the old Geoff, the charming man she'd dated and fallen for.

Before the beast had been unleashed.

His coppery, snake eyes bore into hers, assessing, probing. "You'll be here when I get home tonight?"

She forced a smile, knowing any hint of defiance—or her plans—would set him off. "Of course. I was going to make that prime rib you like for dinner."

"With the little new potatoes and asparagus?"

"Yes. And your favorite cheesecake for dessert."

Relief filled his face. "Good. I'll pick up a bottle of wine."

"That sounds lovely."

He stared at her for another minute, an odd expression flickering in his eyes, and she hoped she hadn't gone overboard with the cheesecake.

Then he stroked her hair from her cheek. "You are such a wonderful wife."

Meaning she was being obedient.

Hopefully for the last time in her life. If she escaped him, she'd never allow another man to order her around. Tell her what to wear. How to fix her hair. How to talk and smile.

How to raise her unborn child.

She watched as he climbed naked from bed and strode into the bathroom to shower. Sinewy muscles and impeccable abs, not an ounce of fat on his lean body, because like everything else, Geoff carried working out to an obsession.

Twenty minutes later, the designer suit he chose indicated the breakfast meeting was important. Probably with another multi-million-dollar client from the law firm.

He thought his wealth and lavish gifts would keep her satisfied.

But she could care less about the money.

She wanted out.

She refused to raise a baby with a father who ruled the house with his fists.

As soon as the door clicked shut and the sound of the alarm dinged that he'd reset it, she rose and showered, forcing herself not to rush in case he forgot his keys or wallet.

Thirty minutes later, adrenaline-spiked and a voice whispered in her head, urging her to hurry. She rushed to her hiding spot, retrieved the cash she'd saved along with the phony ID and the debit card under that name, and raced outside to her car. Once she got out of town, she'd ditch the Toyota and catch a bus out of Austin. From there, she'd take different buses in a zigzag pattern to thwart detection.

Maybe she'd settle in some small town out west. A ranch out in the country where it was quiet and peaceful.

Someplace Geoff would never find her.

She had just closed the trunk and walked back inside to grab the .22 she'd purchased for protection when the kitchen door swung open and Geoff stepped inside. Pistol in hand, she quickly tried to store it in the kitchen drawer, but his disapproving gaze raked over her, and his lips thinned into a straight line.

"Going somewhere, Mia?"

She sucked in a sharp breath. "Just to the market to pick up fresh vegetables for dinner. I thought you had an early breakfast meeting."

A muscle jumped in his cheek as the familiar look of fury darkened his face. "I do. With you."

He suddenly lunged for her, and she knew what was coming.

Panicking, she swung the pistol up. "No, Geoff. Not this time. You're going to let me leave."

A cynical laugh rumbled from his throat. "I will never let you go, Mia."

She pulled the trigger, but it made a clicking sound and no bullet fired. Panic hit her as he dropped the bullets onto the counter.

His eyes narrowed. "You didn't really think you could hide anything from me, did you?" He reached up and twirled a strand of her hair around his fingers. "I'm your husband. You promised to love me forever."

"Geoff, please . . ."

But she never finished the sentence. He drew his fist back and slammed it into her jaw. She staggered backward, the gun flipped from her hand onto the floor, and he grabbed her throat.

Fighting him always made it worse, so she normally cowered and tried to protect her face. But not this time.

Determination kicked in and she struggled, kicking and pulling at his hands. He flung her against the counter, and she managed to open a drawer and grab a knife. She jabbed it at him, but he was stronger, and they wrestled for it.

A blow to her stomach knocked the breath out of her, and she buckled, giving him just enough time to yank the knife from her hand.

One slice to her arm and blood trickled down her wrist. Then he raised the knife and pressed it to her throat.

Fear mingled with rage. God help her.

He was going to kill her before she had a chance to escape.

CHAPTER 1

Six months later

TEXAS RANGER SERGEANT ALEX Townsend scrubbed a hand over his face as he studied the police report on his computer.

```
Three inmates escaped the Huntsville State
Penitentiary when a fire broke out in the
prison a few hours ago.
All three prisoners are considered armed and
extremely dangerous
```

Mugshots appeared on the screen with the inmates' names listed below the photos.

```
Forty-year-old Larry Buckham was serving a
life sentence for murder. Twenty-seven-year-
old Robert Simpleton was on death row for
the brutal slaying of three girls outside of
Austin. And thirty-year-old Geoffrey Jones was
```

serving a fifteen-year sentence for the vicious assault and attempted murder of his
wife Mia.
A statewide manhunt is underway.

Alex's throat tightened. The last man, Geoffrey Jones—that had been Alex's case. The images of Mia's delicate face, bruised and battered from the beating she'd taken from her husband, flashed in his head.

Truth was, the image had haunted him ever since he'd met Mia.

She was petite, barely five-three, with ebony hair that flowed down her back and the biggest chocolate brown eyes he'd ever seen. Eyes that had felt too much pain at the hands of a man who proclaimed to love her.

Fragile as she'd appeared the first time he'd seen her lying in that hospital bed with barely an inch on her that wasn't black and blue, and knife wounds that covered her arms and stomach, she'd turned out to be a courageous little bundle in court.

For once, the justice system had worked. When her lawyer had flashed the photos the police had snapped when she'd been brought into the ER, the jury's reaction had been audible shock.

Thankfully Jones's money, fancy law degree, and charming smile hadn't swayed the jury.

Even the bastard's show of undying love for his wife hadn't fooled them. They'd recognized his declaration of devoted love for what it was—a sick man's obsession and need for control.

They'd found Jones guilty within a half hour after going into deliberation.

Which had pissed off Jones royally. He was accustomed to

always having his way. Living in style. And having others bow to his commands,

Alex stood, swiping his hand down his chin. Dammit. Now the man was loose, he knew exactly where he would go.

To find Mia.

Alex muttered a curse and strode through the bullpen, his hand gripping his phone and checking for Mia's current address as he rushed down the stairs and outside to his car.

The prisoners had escaped the night before around midnight. It was six A.M. now.

Meaning Jones had hours on him. Hours to track down Mia.

He had to hurry.

———

MIA RODE THE CHESTNUT across the Crossties Ranch, Crossties because of the two families who'd joined in marriage after a long family feud. Henry McCauley and his wife Joy were getting up in age and needed help with exercising and training their horses, and she'd jumped at the chance.

She'd never felt freer in her entire life.

No cell phone in her hands at all times in case Geoff needed to know where she was. No one watching over her shoulder like a hawk to make sure she kept the house spic and span. No one forcing her to smile for his friends and then punishing her later because he'd misread a smile as flirtation. No one telling her what she could and couldn't do as if she was a child.

No one reprimanding her for not being the perfect wife.

In fact, horseback riding was one of the things Geoff had hated. And if he hated it, they hadn't done it.

She hadn't been allowed.

If only she'd seen that side of him before the nuptials. But no, he'd been a charismatic gentlemen who'd wooed her with gifts, flowers, fancy dinners and compliments.

Naïve her. Having grown up with a father who'd skipped out when she was two and a mother who'd faded into a booze bottle, she'd been completely snowed by Geoff's attention.

He'd held his deep, dark secret close to the vest until after the honeymoon. Twelve months, twenty-two days and sixteen hours. That's how long their marriage had lasted.

Twelve months, twenty-two days and sixteen hours too long.

Unlike the McCauleys who were going on fifty years now. Such a sweet couple. Joy liked to cook and Henry oversaw the cattle side of the business. At one time, between the ranch hands, cook, and vet they kept on retainer, they'd had nearly a hundred employees. But slowly, Henry had sold off the herd and parcels of land, and now he was down to a dozen ranch hands the cook, and her. She was responsible for exercising and grooming the horses.

A cool spring breeze rustled the trees and sent wildflowers swaying by the pond as she passed. Several Longhorns stood chewing their cud and lazing around the water as if they didn't have a care in the world.

Sunshine glinted off the stones and boulders in the distance, the scent of fresh hay and grass wafting around her as she neared the stables.

The sight of the official-looking Texas Ranger vehicle parked in front of the main house made her breath catch.

Had something happened to make Henry and Joy call the police?

Or ... no ... Geoff was locked away in the state penitentiary. He wasn't eligible for parole for seven years.

But just as she steered the chestnut toward the house, Sergeant Alex Townsend stepped from the vehicle. He tilted his hat and looked at her with those deep, dark assessing eyes, and her heart began to pound.

Her worst fear was that Geoff would somehow get out and come for her. That he would be free again.

His freedom meant hers had come to an end.

And his release was the only reason she could think of for Sgt. Townsend to come here himself.

ALEX SUCKED IN A sharp breath at the sight of Mia riding up on that horse. With the wind blowing her long dark hair around her face, and the sun glinting off her skin, she looked so peaceful.

Happy.

A far cry from the frightened battered woman he'd met in the hospital.

Guilt made his stomach knot.

He was about to rob that peace from her and hoist her back into the world of fear she'd lived with for months.

A frown replaced the contentment he'd seen earlier as she drew the horse to a halt, slid from the animal's back, tied the horse to a hitching post, then walked toward him. He couldn't help but soak in her features and the changes in her. Her once pale skin glowed a golden bronze now from the Texas sun.

And those eyes—before they'd been filled with sadness, anger, the kind of terror no woman should ever experience at the hands of the man who'd vowed to cherish and love her.

For a moment before she'd dismounted and realized he'd been driving that police vehicle, happiness had shimmered in the depths.

Guilt sliced through him because he was about to destroy that happiness.

Still, he couldn't take his eyes off of her. Where she'd been way too thin before, she'd actually gained weight and in all the right places, giving her curves that would make a man's mouth water.

He froze, irritated at his reaction. Mia Matthews had been part of a case he'd worked. A victim for God's sake.

Off limits.

She still was.

Alex had a hard and fast rule about staying single. Kept his emotions intact and his social life, *sex*, separate from the job.

It was safer for everyone that way.

"Sgt. Townsend," Mia said, her voice crisp as if bracing herself for bad news.

He tipped his Stetson, his body humming with anxiety. She didn't deserve to have to live in fear again. "Mia."

The wind tossed strands of her hair around her cheek, and she tucked it behind her ear. His gaze caught on one of the scars on her fingers.

Awareness fluttered through her, and she instantly dropped her hand. "I don't suppose you're here to buy a horse."

He shook his head. "No, I'm sorry."

A heartbeat passed, fraught with tension, then she sighed wearily. "What happened?"

Two ranch hands were riding up. He didn't want to spill the news to her in front of them. "Can we go inside and talk?"

She studied him for a long moment, "Sure. But let's go to my cabin. I think I need to sit down."

He nodded and gestured for her to lead the way. She turned, and he found his gaze glued to her backside. Tight worn jeans hugged her butt, her ponytail swaying as she led him past the stable and down a path by the creek where a small log cabin sat nestled in the woods.

It looked like a postcard picture for a vacation home. A homemade wreath hung on the front door, and colorful flowers swayed in the flowerbeds flanking the rocking chair front porch.

"You're happy here, aren't you?" he asked.

Mia angled her head toward him from the top of the steps. "I love it. It's small but homey and . . . it's mine."

He gave a clipped nod, hating again that he was going to destroy her sense of peace.

She opened the door and ushered him in, then offered coffee. He accepted, stalling the inevitable. She handed him a ceramic hand painted mug that looked as if it had come from one of the reservations nearby.

"If I remember, you take it black," she said softly.

"You have a good memory."

"Some things are hard to forget," she said, a wave of sadness washing over her face. Other emotions flickered there, too, ones he didn't recognize and didn't want to explore.

One night before the trial, she'd broken down, and he'd lost control and wrapped his arms around her. That first touch had set him on fire and scared the crap out of him.

Because he'd wanted her for himself.

After that, he'd been careful not to touch her.

She poured herself a mug of coffee, then claimed the big club chair in the corner by the stone fireplace but she didn't drink the coffee. Instead she seemed to be cradling the cup like a lifeline, as if she needed the warmth to ward off a deep chill.

"Okay, Sgt. Townsend, tell me. Where is he?"

"I don't know," Alex said, his voice grave. "He broke out of prison last night with two other inmates."

Mia's hand shook, sloshing coffee over the rim and onto her hand. He reached out and took the cup from her, then set it on the wooden coffee table. "I'm sorry, Mia. There's a statewide manhunt out for him now."

MIA WAS *HIS*.

She had been from the moment he'd laid eyes on her in that coffee shop. She'd looked so delicate as she'd rushed in, all windblown and sexy with those enormous eyes.

All slender and soft and perfect, like she'd been born to please him.

Flirting with her had come naturally. Making love to her such an innate, desperate need that he'd had to force himself to wine and dine her before taking her to bed.

And then the wedding. Ahh...Mia had no family, no

mother to dote on her or interfere, no father to have to ask for her hand. Isolated and alone, she'd needed him as much as he'd needed her. Giving her the wedding of her dreams had brought him great pleasure just as molding her into the perfect wife had.

The ungrateful bitch.

He snuck into the cheap hotel room, then dropped the hair dye onto the sink. Damn, but he liked his looks and hated like hell to change his appearance.

But doing so was necessary to find the love of his life.

If she thought that being locked in a cell or that distance and time had dimmed his feelings for her, she was sorely mistaken.

In fact, the effect had been quite the opposite. Without his job to focus on, he'd had hours and hours every day to think about her. Remember her.

Imagine the two of them back together again. Sharing the same roof. The same dinner table.

The same bed.

Together they'd stood in front of the preacher and declared their love—till death do us part.

It was time Mia remembered that vow.

CHAPTER 2

H E BROKE OUT OF *prison. He broke out of prison. He broke out of prison.*

The words reverberated over and over in Mia's head like a drum pounding out a war song. She had to swallow to make her voice work. This tough Texas Ranger had seen her at her most vulnerable.

She'd worked too hard to regain her dignity to show him that side again. She could not, *would* not, let this destroy her. "How did it happen?"

Sgt. Townsend sipped his coffee. "Around midnight, one of the prisoners set a fire. Sent alarms peeling. Guards had to move the inmates in that wing. During the process, Jones and two other prisoners jumped the guards, stole their weapons and bulldozed their way out of the building."

Mia contemplated his words, images forming in her head.

When Geoff had first been arrested, she'd had a difficult time imagining how he'd react in prison. Stripped of his personal belongings, his three-piece suits, and Rolex, how would he survive?

Then again, he had money and power on the outside. Why wouldn't he use it to help him inside?

He'd certainly been violent with her. Why wouldn't he turn that violence on the guards who he probably perceived as wronging him?

Geoff could easily have bought contraband, cell phones, and . . . paid someone to track her down.

"Has he been spotted anywhere?" she asked, fighting to calm the desperation in her voice.

Alex shook his head. "We believe the three men split up once they escaped. They stole an employee's car from the parking lot and hightailed it away. That car was found abandoned about a hundred miles away in a discount store parking lot."

"And they did what? Stole more cars?"

"Actually, no cars were reported stolen. We think they had friends on the outside who helped them."

Mia gripped her hands together as if by doing so she could keep herself from falling apart. The image of her ultrasound flashed in her mind.

Then waking up in the hospital to the horrible realization that her baby had died.

She'd begged her lawyer not to reveal that she'd been pregnant at the trial, but Geoff's attorney had learned about the pregnancy from the medical report.

Geoff had accused her of sleeping with someone else and said the baby wasn't his.

But the jurors had seen that unsympathetic side of him, and her attorney had pointed out that if he thought she was having an affair, it provided motive for the vicious attack.

The fact that he hadn't shown remorse for killing his own unborn child had clenched the guilty verdict.

"Geoff had money and friends," she said, disgust rolling through her. "They didn't believe the accusations about him."

"I know. I watched his parents at the trial. They were in denial," Sgt. Townsend said. "Plus, the photographs of your injuries were never released to the public, so it made it easier for his so-called friends to believe him." He heaved a breath. "But at least the jury wasn't dissuaded by his charm."

Humiliation suffused Mia. Thank God for that.

Looking back, she realized she should have left Geoff a lot sooner than she'd tried to. But after each violent outburst, he kept promising that he loved her and would never hurt her.

Now she understood that was the typical pattern of an abuser.

She reached for her coffee and sipped it slowly, then looked out the window at the horses running freely in the pasture.

Yesterday, even this morning, she'd enjoyed that same freedom.

But Sgt. Townsend—no Geoff's escape—had just stolen it from her.

ALEX STUDIED MIA, GIVING her time to absorb the news. She was taking it better than he'd expected. Keeping her composure.

Of course, she could be falling apart on the inside.

But her courage didn't mean she wasn't in danger.

"Pictures of Geoff along with the other inmates are being plastered all over the television news, internet and newspapers. Law enforcement officers across the States are on high alert and are looking for him."

She offered him a tentative smile and placed the coffee back on the table, then knotted her hands to keep him from seeing that they were trembling. "Thanks, Sgt. Townsend. I know you'll find him."

But would it be soon enough?

The idea of Geoff hurting her again made his chest clench.

Alex couldn't help himself. He reached over and covered her hands with his. The same shock of electricity that had sizzled along his nerve endings when he'd held her six months ago shot through him.

She must have felt it, too, because she lifted her gaze to his, alarm flashing in her eyes.

Still, he didn't release her hand. He couldn't let her go through this ordeal alone.

It was his job to protect her. "We will find him, I promise, Mia."

"Meanwhile, he could be on his way here now," she said in a low whisper.

Unable to deny the truth, he shrugged. "He could be. Or maybe he's going to play it smart and head for the border. He knows if he gets caught, he'll go back to prison, and any chance of parole will be history."

Mia's sad shake of her head mirrored his own thoughts. "We both know that he'll come after me," she said. "He said as much at the trial." She pulled her hand away and stood, then walked over to the picture window and stared out at the lush green pasture. "He was obsessed with me. Now he's going to be obsessed with getting revenge. With making me pay for disgracing him."

Alex wanted to argue but there was no use. That would be lying to Mia, and he refused to do that.

But he ached to comfort her, so he walked over and stood behind her, watching the horses and trying to see the land through Mia's eyes. Beautiful rolling hills, wildflowers, horses . . . a peaceful view that was so vastly different from her life with Geoff in his million-dollar estate with its iron fenced gates, state of the art alarm system, and neatly trimmed shrubbery.

"You didn't wrong him, Mia. He was the one who hurt you," Alex said gruffly. "No man should ever lay his hand on a woman like he did."

Mia's shoulders sagged, and she turned to him, her eyes glittering with emotions. "But he sees the world differently," she said matter-of-factly. "In his eyes, I was the one who broke our vows. Who betrayed him by even thinking about leaving."

"He didn't deserve you," Alex said, unable to keep the anger from his voice.

She rubbed her hands up and down her arms as if a sudden chill had swept over her. "In his eyes, he saved me. I was nothing but a small-town girl with no money, no future. He told me once that he would give me the world." A bitter laugh escaped her. "Instead he imprisoned me."

"And gave you a world of hurt," Alex said, his heart-tugging. "I won't let him hurt you again."

"You can't promise that," Mia said. "No one can. If he wants to find me, he will."

"We can take you to a safe house," Alex said. "Give you around the clock protection."

A steely look crossed her angelic face, a combination that he admired and one that stirred primal instincts inside him that he'd never felt before on a case.

And she *was* a case. Just a case.

That's all she could ever be.

"This is my home," she said. "I'm not going to leave it because of him."

"But you aren't safe here."

She shook her head. "Geoff took a lot of things from me during our marriage, but I'm not his wife anymore, and I refuse to let him take me from the place I love."

A war raged in Alex's head. If he put her in a safe house, he could assign different officers to watch her. Then he could spend every minute of every day hunting down the bastard who'd made her life hell.

When he'd first seen her in the hospital, an animalistic rage had taken root inside him, and he'd wanted to give the man a taste of his own medicine.

He'd wanted to kill him.

"If you refuse to go, Mia, I'll assign a man to stay here with you."

Her look turned frigid. "I can't have some strange man following me around. I ... that would be almost as bad as being locked in a house with Geoff."

He made a snap decision, hoping he wouldn't regret it but already doing so before he spoke.

Still, he said what was on his mind anyway, because he

couldn't very well leave her alone. "Then you're stuck with me until he's caught."

———————

MIA COULDN'T HAVE HEARD the Ranger right. *He* was going to stay with her.

No, no, no, that wouldn't work. Although he was the one man she trusted with her life, he was also the only man she'd met since the horrible debacle of her marriage that actually made her stomach flutter with awareness.

Not that he was anything like Geoff with his expensive suits and flashy car. Alex Townsend was the opposite—an alpha male law officer who wore jeans, boots, a hat and a silver star. He was all masculine, muscles and brawn, and had steely gray eyes that had cut through Geoff's façade.

Then looked at her with kindness and compassion.

Pity was more like it.

She'd been a wreck, and he'd helped rescue her from hell. Maybe she'd developed some kind of savior worship complex because he'd been her hero during the worst time of her life.

But God help her, the pure sight of him did something to her insides and stirred longings that she never again would allow herself to indulge in. Still, she could easily see him riding across the ranch, rounding cattle or breaking a wild stallion.

Or kissing her gently and making passionate love to her.

But appearances were deceiving—she'd learned that the hard way. And he hadn't gotten to be a law officer without being tough, without using physical strength to wrangle in criminals.

She didn't think he'd ever use it on a woman, but she hadn't thought Geoff would either.

And she'd been dead wrong . . .

"Mia?"

"I can't let you do that," she said, a note of panic in her voice. "You need to be looking for Geoff."

"I will be," he said. "But I'm also not leaving you unguarded."

"I'll be fine," she said with a defiant tilt to her chin. "He has no idea where I am."

He studied her for a long minute. "I hope that's true. But he could have contacts on the outside. Someone who tracked you down already."

A shudder coursed up her spine. Of course, she knew that was possible. "But I'm miles and miles from Austin in the middle of nowhere."

"You're using your maiden name," he said. "Even a low rent PI could find you through your bank account, debit or credit card."

Mia bit her lip. "I shouldn't have opened an account," she said. "But I thought—"

"You were safe because he was in prison," he finished for her.

She nodded. Unfortunately, the only way she'd ever be safe was if he was dead.

She hated herself for thinking such horrible thoughts. But it was true.

Geoff had sworn that he'd never let her go, that their vows *till death do us part* meant exactly that.

It was only a matter of time until he found her and made her pay.

Sgt. Townsend gestured out the window at the stables. "Do you know all of the employees who work here?"

She frowned. "I've met most of the ranch hands. Henry and Joy, the owners are an older couple and wonderful people. The cook Joleen is in her early sixties and a sweetheart."

"How many ranch hands are there?"

"Ten."

"Any recent hires?"

A frisson of fear darted through her. "New ones?"

He nodded. "Ones who were hired since you came to work here?"

She thought back. "Yes. But—"

"I have to check them out, Mia."

"You think Geoff could have sent one of them here to watch me?"

"I wouldn't put it past him. Right now, we can't rule anything out." He crossed his arms, his western shirt stretching across massive shoulders.

She had the sudden urge to lean into him, to seek solace in his arms. Just for a minute, to alleviate the chill enveloping her and to stop the trembling that had started deep inside her.

"Who else knows you moved here? Any old friends?"

"No." Stupidly she'd alienated herself from everyone once she'd married and realized how controlling and possessive Geoff was. Of course, that had happened slowly, even before she'd known it. He had occupied all her time, made plans for them, swept her away on trips and kept her busy attending society functions for his law firm.

Suddenly she'd realized it had been months since she'd spoken to her old friends. And after the first time, he'd hit her, she'd been too ashamed to turn to anyone.

"If I remember correctly, you didn't have any family?"

"That's right."

"How did you hear about the job here?"

"Through an ad in the paper," Mia said. "The moment I drove out and saw the ranch, I fell in love with it."

"I'll do everything I can to keep you safe here then," he said. "But you have to stay close to me, Mia."

Mia stiffened. She already felt smothered.

"I'll need a list of all the employees," he said. "And I'd like to talk to the ranch owners. They should be aware of the situation."

She nodded, her heart racing. Maybe she'd been selfish in insisting on staying at the Crossties.

What if Geoff showed up and hurt the McCauleys to get to her?

***

Geoff cursed as he sank lower into the car. He needed to talk to his parents. But he had to be careful.

The police would already have a tracer on their phone. And the cops were all over the damn place looking for him.

Dear sweet Maureen and Ross Jones were probably having fits at the sight of his mug shot on the news.

His father had taught him about business and . . . how to be a man.

His mother had made her mistakes over the years, but his

father had been patient and trained her how to be the perfect wife.

He'd hoped Mia would turn out like Maureen. Obedient. Doting. A woman who'd keep a pristine house, keep herself in top shape for him, and pleasure him at his beck and call.

But Mia hadn't been perfect. She'd been weak and careless with her appearance at times. The cupboards were always a mess, the canned goods not alphabetized the way he'd shown her. And he didn't want to think about the way she sometimes let that dark hair go wild and curly.

He liked it clipped in a tidy chignon at the base of her neck.

She *had* been learning though. At least he'd thought she was.

Until he'd discovered her secret stash of money. And that revolver.

Still, every night when he'd closed his eyes as he'd laid on that dump of a prison cot, he saw her face. Her eyes gleaming with admiration and love for him.

He heard her whispered sigh of pleasure as he made love to her.

He would have her again.

There was no doubt in his mind.

And this time she would be his forever.

CHAPTER 3

M IA HATED TO BOTHER the McCauleys, but they needed to be alerted to the possibility that a fugitive might show up at the Crossties. If they wanted her to leave the ranch, she would. They had been too kind to her to think of doing anything but following their wishes.

She knocked on the door of the big farmhouse, rethinking her stubborn insistence about staying.

Maybe she should go to a safe house until Geoff was apprehended.

Alex stood behind her, his gaze perusing the property surrounding the house for trouble.

"I'd like to ride the ranch and scope out the in and out points?"

She frowned. "The in and out points?"

"Spots where Geoff might have easy access to enter the property. Roads nearby. Places where he could hide."

Just the thought of Geoff sneaking onto the ranch and watching her made her stomach revolt.

The door opened, and Joy looked up with a smile, her apron dusted with flour. "Come on in, Mia. And who is this handsome stranger with you?"

"Sgt. Alex Townsend with the Texas Rangers," Mia said, not surprised at the way Joy's face lit up. Obviously, *she* wasn't the only woman immune to Alex's good looks.

"Howdy, Mrs. McCauley," Sgt. Townsend said. "Pleasure to meet you."

Except this wasn't a pleasant social visit.

"Any friend of Mia's is a friend of ours," Joy said, waving them inside. "We just love Mia. She's wonderful with the horses. And a real card shark at Poker. She beats me and Henry every time."

Sgt. Townsend laughed. "She's full of surprises."

Mia inwardly grimaced at the lies she'd told to hide her past. When Henry had asked how she'd gotten so good at the game, she claimed that she'd learned from a college boyfriend. But the truth was that she'd picked up the game by watching her mother and her scam artist boyfriend when she was a little girl.

Joy gestured for them to follow her inside. "Come on and sit down in the kitchen. I just pulled an apple pie from the oven. Would you like a slice?"

"Not for me," Mia said, the very idea of food turning her stomach.

"I'm fine, Mrs. McCauley," Sgt. Townsend said. "But Mia and I need to talk to you."

"This sounds serious," she said, her gray eyebrows knitting.

"It is," Sgt. Townsend said.

"Is Henry here?" Mia asked as Joy led them into the kitchen.

"Yes, he just got back from town."

"Can you ask him to come in here," Mia said. "I really need to speak to both of you."

Worry knitted Joy's expression. "Of course, dear. Just a second." Joy wiped her hands on her apron and disappeared into the hallway off the kitchen which led to the master suite they'd added to the house. Henry had arthritis and they decided they were tired of climbing stairs.

Mia stewed over the situation while they waited, but Sgt. Townsend paced over to the kitchen window, his gaze once again drawn to the outside.

Geoff could be on his way here now. Or . . . he might have already found the ranch and be waiting for the chance to get her alone so he could kill her.

ALEX RARELY TRUSTED ANYONE. Detective work had taught him that.

But he instantly liked the McCauleys, his gut instinct telling him that this kind middle-aged woman and man were not a threat to Mia.

Joy was plump with rosy cheeks and seemed to love baking while Henry was thin with graying hair, a mustache, wore overalls and boots, and bragged about how much he loved working the land. They both insisted he call them by their first names, and that he have a piece of Joy's apple pie.

It was the best pie he'd ever tasted. No little lady who cooked like that could be anything but kind. Could she?

Alex had seen other cases where seemingly sweet old ladies or men turned out to be evil.

He'd have to check the couple's financials. If they needed money for some reason, Geoff could have used his wealth to persuade them to help him. For cripe's sake, the bastard was charming and had convinced all of his friends that Mia had fabricated the spousal abuse charges. He'd even argued in court that she'd paid someone to beat her up, so she could have him arrested and go after his money.

But Mia had adamantly refused to take a dime from him, negating that theory in the minds of the jury.

"So, what's this about?" Henry asked after they'd chitchatted for a moment.

Mia released a weary sigh. "I should have told you this before I moved here."

The couple exchanged concerned looks. "Told us what?" Joy asked.

Anxiety radiated from Mia in waves, making Alex want to reach out and hold her hand, to comfort her.

But he couldn't do that. The couple would get the wrong idea. Hell, Mia might get the wrong idea.

"Two years ago, I married a man named Geoff Jones," Mia said. "He was from a prominent family and was a lawyer in Austin."

The McCauleys simply waited, their hands joined as if bracing themselves for bad news. Which meant that they were either really good actors or that they didn't know about Jones.

"What happened, dear?" Joy asked.

"The marriage turned out to be . . . a disaster," Mia said, a note of derision in her voice. "Geoff was volatile."

Henry dropped his fork on his plate, his eyes narrowing. "He hit you?" Henry asked.

Mia twisted her hands in her lap. "Yes. And when I tried to leave him, it got worse."

She paused as if it pained her to continue, and Alex cleared his throat. "He put her in the hospital," he said, anger vibrating in his voice. "Mia filed charges. Jones was arrested for assault and battery with intent to kill and has been serving time in the State Penitentiary the past few months."

"Has been?" Henry asked, zeroing in on Alex's words.

Mia heaved a weary breath. "Yes. Sgt. Townsend came to tell me that Geoff escaped."

"Oh, my heavens, he was one of those three inmates on the news," Joy said. "They said he was dangerous."

"He is," Alex said. "The police are conducting a statewide manhunt for him and the other two prisoners, but until he's caught, that means that Mia—"

"Is in danger," Henry said, finishing Alex's sentence.

"Exactly."

Joy rose and pulled Mia into a hug. "Oh, honey, I'm so sorry. What an awful ordeal to go through."

Mia accepted her hug, her delicate body trembling slightly with emotions that he sensed she was holding in.

"What can we do to help?" Henry asked matter-of-factly.

"We discussed a safe house, but she refused," Alex replied. "Mia wants to stay here."

"I was just being selfish," Mia said as she pulled away from Joy. "I'll go. I can't stay here and endanger the McCauleys."

"Nonsense," Joy said. "This is your home, Mia. We want you here with us."

"She's right," Henry said in a thick voice. "I've got my rifle. If this man shows up and tries to hurt our Mia, we'll take care of him."

Alex almost smiled at the man's fatherly tone. It appeared that Mia had finally found a family. No wonder she didn't want to leave.

The fact that she'd actually changed her mind and offered to go to the safe house indicated how much she loved these people.

"I'll be staying on as her bodyguard until he's caught," Alex said. "Meanwhile, it would be helpful if you'd let me ride your property, install a security system in her cabin and allow me to see your employee files."

Joy's face turned pinched. "I'm afraid we may not be able to afford the security system."

"Don't worry," Mia said. "I'll cover it."

Alex wondered if she had the money, but they would discuss that later.

"Why do you want to look at our employees?" Henry asked.

Alex didn't want to alarm them, but he had to cover all the bases. "It's routine. Geoff was a wealthy and powerful man. He might have hired someone to find Mia. He could have someone working here as a ranch hand. Or one of your workers might have seen someone suspicious. Did you run background checks on all your men?"

The couple exchanged a concerned look. "Not exactly," Henry said. "We fell on hard times the last few years. My funds have been low, and I had to cut the budget. I just hired men who needed work and didn't mind doing it cheaply."

So, the McCauleys had experienced money problems. That would have made them vulnerable to Geoff if he'd offered them a deal.

But Alex couldn't picture the caring couple turning on Mia. Not even for financial security.

Henry stood. "I'll get that list from my office."

"Thanks." Alex followed him to the door and lowered his voice. "I'd also like your permission to question them."

Henry looked him square in the eye. "You have my permission to do whatever you need to keep that little girl safe. Joy and I never could have kids, but when Mia came along, it was like God sent her. We knew something was wrong. She looked fragile, like this little dog we once had that had been mistreated. Now we understand the reason."

Alex nodded, agreeing with the image. "She certainly looks happy here, Henry. I want to see her stay that way."

They shared an understanding look, then Alex trailed Henry to his office and watched as the man sat down at his ancient computer, accessed the file and hit *print*.

Alex skimmed the names as he took the list, zeroing in on the most recent hires.

Truitt Wilson and Emmett Royce.

He'd run an extensive background check on each of them as soon as he got back to his computer.

But at first glance, his suspicions rose. Truitt Wilson was

from Austin, Geoff Jones's hometown.

They could have some connection, and Geoff could have sent Wilson after Mia.

MIA'S NERVES WERE ON edge as Sgt. Townsend returned from Henry's office. Joy's kindness had made her feel even more guilty for not going to a safe house.

If anything happened to her or Henry, she'd never forgive herself.

"Henry," Joy said as her husband walked in. "Maybe we should call a meeting of all the hands and tell them to be on the alert for strangers on the ranch."

"Good idea," Henry said. "Sgt. Townsend, do you have a picture of this man, Jones, so we can show it around?"

"Sure, I'll bring it to the meeting," the Ranger said. "I want to watch the men's reactions when you tell them what's going on."

"Fair enough. Give me a second and I'll call the foreman and set it up. Most of the men are out working now. We're moving the cattle from the north pasture to the east, so it'll be hard to reach them at the moment. How about around dinner time?"

"That's fine," Alex said. "Thank you for your cooperation."

Mia hugged them both. "I'm sorry to put you in this situation."

Joy patted Mia's back. "We love you, Mia. We just want to make sure you're safe."

Mia's heart tugged painfully. The McCauleys might not have

much money, but they were wealthy with love. They were good people and had been kinder to her than anyone she'd ever known.

"If I find out he's here, I'll leave," Mia said. "I won't let him hurt you or Henry."

Joy patted her hands. "We are family, Mia. If he hurts you, he hurts us."

Mia's throat closed. She hugged Joy, then she and Alex walked out together. "I'm going to investigate the men on this list before we talk to them," he said. "But first I want to have a chat with the Joneses. Then we'll come back and ride the property and meet with the ranch hands."

Mia bit her lip. Maureen and Ross Jones hated her.

She was surprised they hadn't actually hired someone to kill her themselves.

———

GEOFF GRIPPED THE PREPAID cell phone in his hand as he huddled inside the deserted building. Dammit.

Mia should never have put him in this position. He'd been well respected, a man of power and authority.

To have to hide and run like a common criminal was inexcusable.

She would pay for ruining his reputation.

He had half a mind to go after the jurors who'd convicted him—how Mia had managed to persuade them he was anything, but the perfect husband still astounded him—but doing that could get him caught before he had the opportunity to find his wife.

And finding her was more important.

The private investigator he'd hired, Dennis Sars, answered on the third ring. "Sars speaking."

"Do you have an address for my wife?"

Papers rattled in the background. Something that sounded like an out of date fax machine whirred. "Yes. She's been living and working on the Crossties Ranch about a hundred miles from Austin."

Geoff gritted his teeth. What was his beautiful wife doing there—mucking stalls? The very idea that she'd choose that lifestyle over being *his* wife brought his rage brimming to the surface.

He scribbled the address on a piece of paper, then tucked it into the pocket of his jeans. As soon as he reached his final destination, he'd throw these clothes away and wear something more suitable to his station in life.

But for now, he had to blend in. And if he wanted to go undetected on this damn ranch, he'd have to dress the part. Fury railed through him at having to stoop so low, but even jeans and a flannel shirt were better than prison attire.

He would never go back there.

Never.

He assured the PI he would receive his payment promptly, determined to keep the man on good terms in case he needed him again. And he had paid him well for his confidentiality.

Everyone had a price.

Except Mia.

The bitch.

His emotions for her ping-ponged back and forth between unadulterated love and pure hatred.

Keeping the baseball hat low on his head, he ducked into the small saddle shop, chose a black Stetson, black western shirt, boots with silver studs and a belt buckle with a bull on it. He paid the man cash, carefully avoiding eye contact, his gaze tracking the country store for other patrons who might recognize him.

Thankfully the place was nearly deserted, and the old timer behind the counter had such thick glasses that he was probably half blind.

He carried his purchases outside, then ducked into the restroom around back and changed. When he emerged, the Stetson sitting low on his head, he looked like any other Texas cowboy. Or maybe a country and western singer.

Not the astute lawyer he was.

Mia had robbed him of that.

But new identities in another country, and soon he'd be living the pampered lifestyle he was meant to live.

He jumped in the old pick-up truck one of his fellow inmates who'd been paroled had arranged for him, knowing that would be the last vehicle Mia would expect him to be driving.

He punched in his father's private mobile number, then started the engine and let it idle while the phone rang.

Seconds passed, and two more cars pulled into the parking lot while he waited. Finally, his father answered. "Geoff, are you okay?"

Hell, no he wasn't. He'd been stripped of his life. "Yes. Do you have the bank accounts set up?"

"Yes," his father replied. "But I'm worried, Geoff. The police are all over the place looking for you."

A tense second passed. "Just stay calm and tell them you haven't heard from me. I already have the passports and IDs. As soon as I get Mia, we'll be out of the country."

His father wheezed a breath. "But, Geoff, they're saying on the news that you're dangerous, that the police have orders to shoot to kill."

Before he could comment on his father's statement, his father cursed. "Dammit to hell, son, they're here now."

Fuck. "Who is it?"

"I'm looking out the side window. Shit. It's that same Texas Ranger who handled the case before. And that bitch of a wife of yours is with him."

Rage heated Geoff's blood. "Get rid of them, Dad. And remember, stay cool. You haven't seen or heard from me."

"Geoff, please, you may want to rethink this. I don't want to see you end up dead."

"If anyone's going to die," he growled, "it's going to be Mia."

But he wouldn't kill her right away. He would make her suffer first.

CHAPTER 4

MIA FIDGETED IN THE seat as Sgt. Townsend parked in front of the Jones's estate.

"You don't have to go in if you don't want to, Mia."

She clenched the edge of the seat, fighting her emotions. Trepidation over seeing the couple who'd openly despised her at the trial warred with pride. She had worked hard to overcome the past and vowed that no one would ever make her feel inferior again. And that she'd never be in the position of letting another person lord over her—or make her run.

That not only included Geoff but his parents. When she'd first pressed charges, they'd done everything possible to persuade her to drop the case. Everything from offering her money to intimidation tactics.

If she'd had any family, they would have probably threatened them to twist her arm.

But she had stuck to her guns, and she intended to show them that she wasn't afraid of them.

"No, I need to do this." She lifted her chin. "They made me out to be a conniving gold digger during the trial. They can't do anything else to hurt me."

He gave her an encouraging smile. "You're strong, Mia. Brave. I'm glad you stood up to them."

"I didn't have much of a choice," she said. If she'd gone back to Geoff, she'd eventually have ended up dead anyway.

"How do you plan to approach them, Sergeant?" she asked.

"With the truth," he said bluntly. "And Mia, please call me Alex. We're going to be spending a lot of time together. Sergeant sounds too formal."

Her stomach fluttered. Maybe she needed that formality to keep her distance. Using his first name sounded too . . . intimate.

Like he might be a friend . . . or a lover.

She couldn't afford to think of him that way. She needed a reminder that he was a Texas Ranger, that the only reason he was here was because of his job.

"Mia, are you all right?"

She nodded. "Let's just get this over with."

He gave a small lopsided smile, and her heart stuttered. Please don't look at me like that, she pleaded silently. *Not like I'm a delicate flower you want to protect.*

Or hold.

Because if he tried to touch her, she might just collapse into his arms.

Thankfully oblivious to her thoughts, he opened the car door, and they walked up the brick path to the front door of the

English Tudor mansion. A maid answered the doorbell, scowling when Alex introduced himself.

The older Hispanic woman recognized Mia immediately and averted her eyes as if she didn't know what to say to her. Mia had always wondered if the servants in the house knew about Geoff's violent tendencies. If so, they'd probably been paid well for their silence.

Esmeralda offered them coffee or tea, but they both declined. Ten minutes later, her bravado slipped as Mrs. Jones walked in, her features rigid with hatred. Mr. Jones followed, his scathing look cutting her to the bone.

"What are you doing here?" Mrs. Jones asked, her bracelets clanging as she pointed at Mia.

"You know why I came," Mia said.

Alex cleared his throat. "Please sit down, Mr. and Mrs. Jones. We need to talk about your son."

"He should never have been locked in that horrid place," Mrs. Jones said, her voice vibrating with contempt.

Disapproval hardened Mr. Jones's already icy look. "My wife is right."

"Your son was found guilty by a jury of his peers," Alex said. "But we aren't here to debate his innocence or guilt. He and the two other prisoners who escaped physically attacked and murdered two guards, putting three others in the hospital. Geoff is a wanted felon, and when he's caught, and he *will* be caught, if he resists arrest, officers will shoot to kill."

Mrs. Jones's face drained of color, making Mia almost feel sorry for her. She looked thinner than ever, her cheeks almost gaunt, dark circles beneath her eyes that even her expensive makeup couldn't hide.

Had the woman been in such deep denial about her son that she really hadn't believed he'd caused Mia's injuries?

Of course, she'd spoiled him rotten when he was young. She also lived vicariously through him and his accomplishments.

Geoff's father was as controlling, rigid, and demanding as Geoff had been. She'd read enough about spousal abuse to see that Mrs. Jones had been battered all her life. She probably believed her son was being a good husband as hers had been.

That his job was to train Mia to be the perfect wife.

Mr. Jones smoothed down his tie, his voice curt. "Sgt. Townsend, if my son is injured, I will hold you personally responsible."

"Your son chose to escape, putting himself in harm, so if you blame anyone for his predicament, blame him." Alex steepled his hands. "Which is the reason I'm here. Did you know of his plans to escape?"

"Of course not," Mrs. Jones said. "We were putting together an appeal to get that bogus conviction overturned."

"Mrs. Jones," Mia cut in. "The conviction was not bogus. Your son assaulted me and almost killed me. I have the scars to prove it."

"You're lying," Mr. Jones snapped. "My son is smart and charming. You're a whore who just wanted his money."

Mrs. Jones stood, her narrow jaw set firmly. "You're not welcome in this house, Mia. You should be the one in jail for filing false charges and maligning my son's reputation."

"He maligned it when he sliced open my stomach and I almost bled to death," Mia said. When he killed their unborn baby.

"Sit down, Mrs. Jones." Alex turned to Geoff's father, interrupting a rebuttal from the older man. "Have you heard from your son, Mr. Jones?"

The man shot Alex a cool look. "No. He's too smart to call here. He knows you're probably monitoring our phones and house."

Mia glanced at Alex, wondering if that was true or if he needed a warrant.

Alex narrowed his eyes. "Did *you* know about his plans to escape?"

"Of course not," Mr. Jones said. "I would have persuaded him to wait until this appeal came through."

He sounded awfully confident. Perhaps he'd paid off a judge.

But if so, why hadn't Geoff waited instead of risking his life in a prison break?

"I hope you're telling the truth," Alex said. "Because if I find out you helped your son escape or assisted him in any way, I will arrest you for aiding and abetting a felon."

Mr. Jones shot to his feet and gestured toward the door. "Now, Sergeant, it's time you left. And if you know what's good for you, you won't bring that woman back here again."

"That sounds like a threat," Alex said tersely.

In spite of her best efforts, a shiver rippled up Mia's spine. It had been a threat and everyone in the room knew it. During the trial and even afterward, the couple had crucified her in the media. They'd actually hired a man to intimidate her, but Alex had caught the man. That act had only made things worse for Geoff.

Alex glanced Geoff's mother. "If you don't want your son hurt, Mrs. Jones, I suggest you convince him to turn himself in. If you don't and he's injured or killed, his death will be on your conscience, not mine."

———————

ALEX STORMED OUT OF the Jones's house with Mia close beside him. He'd known questioning them would probably be a waste of time, but he'd had to try.

Mrs. Jones was obviously terrified for her son. But she was more afraid of her husband. The asshole threw his power and money around as if he was God and everyone else should bow to him and had taught his son to do the same.

"Do you think they've spoken to Geoff?" Mia asked when the door slammed behind them.

"Absolutely," Alex said. "Mr. Jones may act cool, but he has a tell."

"What is it?"

"He scratches his temple with one finger. I watched him during the trial and picked up on it."

"But they're going to protect Geoff," Mia said as she climbed into his SUV.

He shrugged. "Protecting him would mean cooperating with us to save his life. Because if he lays a hand on you, I'll kill the bastard."

Mia fastened her seatbelt. "I never wanted him hurt," she said softly. "I just wanted to get away from him."

Alex pulled onto the road. Mia was amazing. Even after all

the pain and suffering, Geoff had put her through, she wasn't vindictive. "You said in the trial that he didn't know about the baby ahead of time. Do you think it would have made a difference?"

Pain wrenched her face, making him regret the question. "No." She fidgeted and glanced back at the house for a moment. "Maybe. Although he was insanely jealous. More than once, he accused me of sleeping around."

His gaze met hers. He refused to ask.

"And no, I never did," she said firmly. "But if a man, even one of his friends who he wanted to impress, smiled at me, he flew into a rage later that night and accused me of flirting."

"Some people think abusers need psychiatric help," he said darkly. "But any man who beats up on a woman is nothing but a low-down coward."

A strained silence fell between them as they drove. Alex wanted to comfort Mia, remind her that none of this was her fault, but his phone buzzed, and he saw it was his superior, so he snatched it up.

"Townsend, it's Chief Dunn."

"Any word on the prison escape?"

"Cantrell is in charge of the search for Larry Buckham and I've put Deke Mann on the Simpleton investigation. He has a lot of experience with serial killers. Any news on Jones?"

Alex relayed his conversation with Jones's parents. "I think they've talked to him, but they'll never admit it. Have the tech team analyze their financials. They probably set up funds for Geoff in an offshore account somewhere."

"All three of them may already have fake ID and passports

to aid them in leaving the country," Chief Dunn said. "We've alerted bus and train stations, airports, the border patrol as well as the cruise lines."

Alex gritted his teeth. Geoff had enough money that he could hire a private jet.

"He'll come for Mia first." Alex's jaw tightened at the sliver of fear that slanted Mia's mouth.

"We've already pulled the Jones's phone records," Chief Dunn said. "So far nothing suspicious on the home line or Jones's cell, but we're still hunting."

"They're probably using prepaid cells," Alex said. "Geoff Jones was a lawyer. He's smart and would have known the police would examine his phone records and financials along with his parents' for suspicious activity."

Still, they had to search.

"How about Jones's cellmate?" Alex asked.

"The FBI has sent in a team to interrogate the inmates to find out exactly what happened and how the men orchestrated the escape."

"Hell, the inmates are so ingenious they can make shanks out of anything," Alex said. And contraband was easier to get than anyone could imagine.

"Tell me about it. They've had five murders at that prison in the last two months. The prison is on full lockdown now pending a massive investigation."

"I'm on my way back to the ranch where Mia works," Alex continued. "There are a couple of new hired hands that I want to talk to. And I might pay a visit to the prison myself. In spite of the friends Jones bought, he probably made a few enemies."

"Good idea." They agreed to stay in touch, and Alex lapsed into silence as he drove back to the Crossties.

When they arrived at the ranch, he scanned the property as they drove past the welcome sign that had been carved into two pieces of wood shaped like a railroad crossing sign. He hadn't ridden the property yet, but he could already tell there were way too many ways to sneak onto this place and get to Mia.

"I need to exercise a couple of the horses before dinner," she said.

"Saddle them up while I check my computer and we'll ride out together. Then we can meet up with the ranch hands for questioning."

She nodded. "I can't let Geoff run my life again, Alex."

"No, but you also have to be realistic, Mia. He will come for you, so we have to be ready."

Resignation flickered in her eyes, but she didn't comment.

He parked and climbed out, then grabbed his laptop and started around the front of the car to open her door, but she'd already slid from the seat and was heading up the porch.

Just as he stepped up behind her, she suddenly tensed and gasped.

"What is it, Mia?"

She gestured toward the door with a shaky hand, and he moved up beside her and saw a bouquet of lilies sitting in front of the door.

He knelt to pick up the card, his anger flaring at the words scribbled on the outside.

"I know what it says," she whispered in a tortured voice. "Nobody loves you like I do."

He glanced down at the card. She was right. He'd heard Jones say those very words to her in court. But instead of sounding affectionate, they held a creepy, sinister tone.

"He told me that over and over during our marriage," Mia whispered.

And it was the last thing he'd said to her right before he'd beaten her and killed their child.

HE WATCHED THE TEXAS Ranger standing beside Mia on the porch, a surge of rage heating his blood. That was the same damn lawman who'd been with her in court.

The same one who'd fastened handcuffs around him and hauled him to jail like he was some two-bit nobody.

And now here he was with Mia. Doing what?

The fucker had probably come to tell her that her loving husband was out of prison.

Or had the asshole been seeing her the entire time he'd been in jail? The Ranger had acted possessive of her during the trial. Possessive and protective and a little too ... cozy, always standing beside her, touching her back, keeping her away from *him*.

Hell, Sgt. Townsend had probably crawled into her bed the minute they'd closed the cell door on Geoff.

Mia backed away from the flowers as the Ranger carried them to the side of the cabin and tossed them into the trash.

What the fuck right did that Ranger have to throw away the flowers *he* had sent Mia? What right did he have to touch *his* wife?

If Mia thought that piece of paper negated their vows, she was wrong. She was his wife. Always had been.

Always would be.

And no one would take her away from him again.

CHAPTER 5

MIA TRIED TO SUPPRESS a shudder at the sight of the lilies and card but failed. By themselves, the items didn't look daunting. Or dangerous.

But Geoff's love had come with strings.

And those flowers and the card meant that he'd found her.

"Son of a bitch," Alex said. "He's ballsy. He wants us to know he's been here."

Mia nodded, too breathless with fear to say anything else. How had he found her so quickly? Had someone been watching her all these months? Someone Geoff had hired?

Had her sense of freedom and safety simply been a figment of her imagination?

Alex took her arm. "Sit down on the swing, Mia. You look pale."

She did feel faint. Damn Geoff. She hated feeling powerless. Afraid.

She thought all that was in the past.

"Mia?" Alex said as he guided her to the swing. "I promise you I won't let him hurt you."

She raised her gaze to his, numb. "You don't know Geoff like I do. When he wants something, he'll do anything to get it."

"He's a bully." Alex stroked her arms. "But I'll stop him. I swear it."

Regardless of all the strides she'd made in her recovery, unwanted tears pooled in her eyes. Geoff would kill anyone who got in his way.

What if he hurt Alex?

Alex exhaled, a battle warring in his eyes as if he wanted to comfort her but knew he shouldn't. But he pulled her up against him anyway and wrapped his arms around her. At first, her body went rigid.

She couldn't lean on him now.

Once Geoff was caught, he'd leave, and she'd be on her own again.

She couldn't afford to lose her heart to another man.

The last time she had, it had ended in disaster and pain.

But Alex murmured nonsensical words of comfort, and in spite of her fierce effort at self-control, her body betrayed her by trembling.

"He's not going to hurt you this time, Mia," Alex whispered against her ear. "I swear, I'll kill him before I let him touch you."

Unable to resist, she gave into his tender caress and closed her eyes. Alex felt so warm and gentle, big and strong, yet his fingers stroked her back in a soothing gesture that made her slowly begin to relax. His heart was beating steadily, his chest rising in slow breaths, the scent of raw man and his aftershave wafting around her.

Geoff was gentle at first. Before you discovered the monster beneath the surface.

She hated the fear that shot through her at the memory. At the knowledge that even though she wanted to trust Alex, that she didn't trust herself, her own judgment.

She'd been so wrong before.

The image of the ultrasound that she kept hidden in her dresser drawer taunted her. God, she hated Geoff.

But she'd wanted that baby.

And he'd taken it away from her just as he'd stolen her pride . . .

So, she slowly pulled away. "I'm sorry, Sgt. Townsend."

He traced a finger along her jaw. "Alex," he corrected her.

She looked into his eyes. His mouth was only a fraction of an inch from hers. His lips curved, promising to soothe her pain.

But she couldn't accept his comfort, so she didn't respond. Saying his name while she could still feel his warm body and hear his promises would be dangerous to her heart.

And she had to protect her heart because falling for Alex would be way too easy.

And a big mistake. She had enough regrets to last a lifetime.

She didn't need another.

———•—————

WHAT THE HELL WAS he doing?

Fear and regret flashed in Mia's eyes, and Alex wished he hadn't touched her. But he couldn't stop himself.

Something about the woman drew him to her, made him want to fight her battles.

She was so lovely, and in spite of how she viewed herself, she was strong. That gutsy side of her made him admire her even more.

"I'm sorry, Mia. I—"

"Do you think he's been inside?" she asked, cutting off his apology.

Dammit. He should have been thinking about that possibility instead of hauling her up against him. But Mia made his head swirl with emotions that played havoc with his common sense.

And his ability to focus.

He *had* to focus to keep her safe.

He instantly removed his weapon, motioned for her to remain in the swing then jiggled the doorknob. It was locked. Mia fished out her keys and handed them to him.

"Is there a back door?"

She nodded. "Off the kitchen."

Of course, he could have broken in through a bedroom window. Alex slipped down the porch steps and walked around the side of the house. He checked the windows, but they didn't look disturbed, then he eased around the back, his gaze scanning the property in case Geoff was waiting to ambush him. The back door was closed, so he tried the knob. Locked. The lock didn't appear to have been picked either.

But he had to be careful. He had no idea what kind of skills Jones had picked up in prison.

Gun at the ready, he inched to the other side of the cabin, noting two windows. Both closed, glass intact.

It didn't mean Jones hadn't gotten inside though.

He hurried back to the front porch, relief filling him when he found Mia sitting in the same spot. Her eyes were wide, glued to the hill in the distance as if she might have seen something.

"Mia?"

She jerked her gaze to his. "Did you see anything?"

"No, did you?"

The keys rattled as she held out her hand to him. "I'm not sure. There might have been someone on horseback at the top of the hill. But it could have been one of the ranch hands."

Or it could have been Jones hanging around to see her reaction when she received his little gift.

Bastard.

He deserved to die.

MIA COULD HAVE SWORN she'd seen Geoff on the hill.

Then again, now that she knew he was near, she'd probably be seeing him in every shadow and corner.

Was he still on the ranch?

"Call Henry and tell him that Jones has been here. As soon as I check the inside of the house we're going to ride the property."

Mia nodded, dug out her cell phone and punched Henry's

number while Alex let himself inside the cabin. From her vantage point on the porch, everything appeared to be as she'd left it. The lights were off. Furniture in place.

The phone rang once, twice, a third time, then Henry answered. Mia quickly explained that Geoff had been on the ranch.

"I'll alert my foreman immediately," Henry said. "I called a meeting of the hands at the chow hall, but I didn't tell them why I wanted to talk to them. Thought if someone was working for your ex, it might tip our hand."

"Good thinking," Mia said, surprised at Henry's forethought. "We'll see you soon. Alex and I are going to take a ride before we meet you. I want to exercise the horses." And she and Alex could look for traces of Geoff.

"Listen, Mia, don't worry about your job until this maniac is caught," Henry said. "Your safety is more important than anything."

Touched by his concern, she blinked back tears and thanked him. But she took her job seriously and cared about the animals, and she wouldn't allow Geoff to prevent her from doing that job.

A second later Alex returned. "The cabin is clean. But you may want to see if anything is missing."

"All right." Not that Geoff would have reason to steal anything of hers. But she'd feel better if she checked.

Her stomach fluttered with nerves as she entered. She quickly scanned the living room and adjacent kitchen but saw nothing amiss. Next, she glanced inside the bathroom. Nothing out of place.

Well, technically things were since she'd rebelled against Geoff's obsessive-compulsive tendencies to have everything perfectly in order and kept a basket on the counter with her cosmetics piled in it. He had insisted they be arranged in order of height on the shelf he'd built strictly for that purpose.

The bedroom looked just as she'd left it as well. Her clothes hanging in the closet. A pair of work boots tossed in the corner. Her denim jacket draped over the chair.

But when she opened her dresser drawer, her lungs constricted. All the sensible underwear that she'd bought was gone.

In its place were delicate lacy bras and thongs, ones like Geoff had bought her.

Ones he'd obviously chosen for her just as he'd insisted on doing so when they were married.

She'd thought it was a romantic gesture at first. Titillating even.

Until it had become suffocating.

When she'd refused to wear the black satin undies he'd given her one night, he'd become enraged and beaten her senseless. That was the first time.

But it hadn't been the last.

Fury raged through her, and she grabbed the trashcan, snatched the lacy garments and hurled them into the garbage.

Alex caught her arm and gently rubbed his thumb along her wrist. "What's wrong, Mia?"

"He was here," she cried. "He bought all of this. None of it is mine."

It was a statement from Geoff. She understood perfectly.

He wanted her to know that he'd found her. And that eventually, he would wear her down.

"Son of a bitch." Alex hooked his thumb toward the door. "I need to check the property now in case he's still lurking around."

She dumped the last of the underwear, fighting a hysterical cry as she faced him. "I'll get the horses ready."

Not without him, she wouldn't. "Then let's go."

"I thought you wanted to run those background checks first."

"Now Jones has found you, I'm not going to let you out of my sight for a minute."

A deep wariness darkened her eyes, but she didn't argue. "Okay, let's go look for him."

He followed her outside, his senses alert as he scanned the area. It would be just like the bastard to stay close and watch Mia.

As they descended the porch, he scanned the area for evidence as to how Jones had reached the cabin. "No tire prints," he said. "The son of a bitch must have parked off the road and hiked in." He glanced at Mia. "Does he ride?"

She shook her head. "No, he doesn't like animals. Too dirty."

"He could have borrowed or stolen one of the ranch hand's horses. Do they keep them in the barn near you?"

"No," Mia said. "There's another stable near the bunkhouses for the workers. The ones I exercise are being groomed to sell."

They crossed the pasture and entered the stable together, and she headed into the tack room for saddles.

He saddled one horse while she saddled the other, and in minutes, they were prepared to ride. Alex snapped his reins and led the way across the pasture toward the hill where she thought she'd seen someone earlier. As they rode, he searched the ground for hoof prints. Boot prints. Any sign of Jones.

When they made it to the top of the hill, he paused, dismounted and studied the ground. A partial boot print marred the dirt, the horse's hoof prints muddying the soil. "Someone was here," he said.

Mia's face looked pained. "There's a petal from one of the lilies," she said in a haunted tone.

Suddenly a shot rang out, the horses bucked and whinnied, and Alex shouted for Mia to get down.

CHAPTER 6

MIA DOVE FROM THE horse then hit the ground on her hands and knees. Who the hell was shooting at them?

A gun wasn't Geoff's style.

But he was desperate and would do anything to get back at her for destroying his life.

And exposing him for the monster he was.

"Stay low," Alex murmured as he covered her head with his body.

She nodded, her breath rasping out.

Alex pulled his gun, lifted his head from their perch on the ground, scanning the area where the shot had come from. To the right, not far from them. Near the woods.

He pointed toward a cluster of rocks a few feet away. "Take cover there. I'm going after the son of a bitch."

She caught his arm. "Be careful, Alex."

He squeezed her hand in reassurance, then led her to the

rocks. The two of them stayed low, Alex covering them by firing a round at the woods.

When she'd crouched behind the boulder, he shocked her by dropping a kiss into her hair. "As soon as I'm gone, ride back to the McCauley's. If I'm not back in half an hour, call the local sheriff. I've already talked to him. He knows what's going on. He'll get in touch with my chief."

Fear nearly choked her. "Alex—"

"Just do it," he said. Then he was gone. Diving on his horse and racing in the direction of the shooter.

She held her breath, anxiety warring with guilt. Alex had been the only one to protect her, to listen to her cries at night during those first few weeks after the arrest.

The only person she'd connected with.

And that had terrified her.

So, when the trial had ended, and Geoff was locked away, she'd cut all ties to the handsome Ranger for her own sake.

Ironic that now he might die to protect her from the one man who claimed he loved her.

At one time she'd been thrilled to have that love. A happily-ever-after in a dreamland that he'd created for her.

Now she didn't believe that happily-ever-after existed. At least not for her.

The loss of her unborn child was proof of that.

Her fingernails dug into the rocks. Why was God punishing her? What had she done so wrong? Been blinded by Geoff's charm and power?

She hadn't thought she was that shallow, but maybe she had been.

Not anymore.

Survival was the only thing that mattered.

Love was for others. People without a past.

Dust rose in a thick cloud behind the horse as Alex disappeared over the hill. She froze in silent prayer, listening for sounds of more gunshots. One. Two.

Had someone been shot?

Terrified, she jumped on her horse, snapped the reins and steered the animal back toward the McCauley's farmhouse.

She just prayed that Alex caught Geoff and didn't lose his life over her.

She couldn't live with herself if he did.

———————

ALEX KICKED THE HORSE'S sides, urging him to go faster as he fired at the shadow in the woods. But the figure moved too quickly, and he missed the shot. The sound of racing hoofs across the terrain splintered the air, his determination to catch the shooter warring with common sense.

He shouldn't have left Mia alone. If this was a trap and the shooter was a distraction, he'd left her vulnerable for Jones's attack.

Dammit.

Another shot zinged by his head and he ducked, guiding the horse to the right to cut through the woods. But the thicket of trees slowed him down, and the shooter disappeared in the distance.

A noise on the opposite side caught his attention, and he

spotted another figure running toward the road that bordered the ranch.

Seconds later, the sound of a motor firing up rent the air, tires squealing on pavement. Reality hit him.

There were two of them.

The road provided easy access for Jones or a hired shooter to slip onto the land while another shooter had been in the woods on horseback.

He steered the bay to the left in search of the vehicle, but by the time he reached the edge of the road, it was gone. Pivoting, he steered the horse toward the man on horseback, weaving between the trees until he reached the clearing. The horse had disappeared as well.

Dammit.

Frustrated but resigned the shooter had escaped, he turned and headed back toward Mia.

Relief filled him as he spotted hoof prints heading toward the farmhouse. Hopefully Mia had made it back safely.

He kicked the bay's sides, sending the animal galloping across the property. His pulse slowed as he approached, his breath finally steadying when he saw Mia's horse tied to the hitching post.

He secured his ride, then climbed the porch steps, angry the shooter had escaped and desperate to see Mia.

He didn't like that feeling of desperation.

But he couldn't help himself. Another few inches, and the shooter could have killed her.

Except now that he thought about it, the bullet had come closer to him than her.

Shit. The shooter *was* firing at him. Hoping to get him out of the way so he could have Mia to himself.

That wasn't going to happen.

At least not as long as he was alive.

MIA'S HEART WAS HAMMERING so hard she thought it would explode. Dear God, if anything happened to Alex, she'd never forgive herself.

"Honey, I'm sure he'll be all right," Joy said as she handed Mia a cup of tea. Mia sank into the wooden chair at the kitchen table, her legs giving way. The woman had been doting on her like a mother hen ever since Mia had run in the door frantic.

"I can't believe this is happening," Mia said, her throat strained from holding back tears. "Geoff has been here. I have to leave."

"You're not leaving," Joy said. "We'll hire extra security to cover the ranch. And Henry's already called about installing a security system."

The teacup rattled in the saucer as she set it on the table. The McCauleys didn't have the money for extra security any more than they had it for a security system. They needed every penny to keep the ranch afloat.

Maybe she should have killed Geoff instead of trying to run from him. At least then he couldn't hurt anyone else.

She wrung her hands together, then froze at the sound of a loud knock on the door. Joy twisted her hand in her apron and glanced toward the hallway leading to the foyer.

"This man after you, he wouldn't knock," Joy pointed out.

Mia released a shaky breath. Joy was right. She rose and hurried to the door, relief flooding her when she spotted Alex standing on the other side. His dark eyes looked intense, his jaw hard, his big body so handsome and virile that her heart fluttered with longing.

Alex had offered her support during the worst time of her life, and he was here for her now.

She swung the door open and threw her arms around him. "Thank God you're all right."

He drew her into a hug, burying his head into her hair. "Thank God you are."

A nervous laugh bubbled in her throat. "I was terrified when you rode off," she whispered.

He framed her face with his hands and looked into her eyes. "I'm fine but he got away."

"Was it Geoff?"

"I didn't get a look at his face," Alex said. "In fact, there were two of them. One on horseback, the other escaped in a car."

Behind her, Mia heard Joy's soft sigh. She pulled away from Alex, knowing how it must look to her friend.

"What happened?" Joy asked. "Did you catch him?"

"I'm afraid not."

A worried look pulled at Joy's brows. The phone jangled, and Joy startled, then rushed to get it. "Yes?" A pause. "Oh, dear Lord."

Her hand trembled as she reached for the bannister by the table holding the phone. "Yes, the Texas Ranger is here. I'll tell him."

Mia's pulse clamored as Joy hung up the phone. When Joy looked up at them, tears clouded her eyes.

Mia released Alex and rushed toward Joy. "What's wrong?"

Joy's lower lip quivered. "It's Joleen . . . Henry found her."

Alex cleared his throat. "What do you mean, found her?"

A sob escaped Joy, and she wrapped her arms around her middle. Mia helped her to the bench against the wall. "She's dead," Joy cried. "Joleen . . . she was murdered."

Panic and guilt slammed into Mia. Had the cook been killed because of her?

Call the sheriff," Alex said. "I'll ride over and meet him at the scene."

Mia's face turned a pasty white. "How did she die, Joy?"

Guilt darkened Mia's expression, making Alex angry all over again. But this case was too important for him to let his emotions rule his actions. And time was of the essence.

"Henry said she was shot at the chow hall," Joy said in a broken voice.

"Oh, my God," Mia whispered. She turned to Alex, panic streaking her face. "You think the same man who shot at us killed Joleen?"

"I don't know." He checked his weapon. "We'll need the ME to establish time of death. And we'll compare bullet casings to the one that killed Joleen."

"This is all my fault," Mia cried. "I never should have come here."

"Don't do that to yourself, Mia," Alex said sharply. "We don't know that this has anything to do with you."

"Of course, it does," she shrieked. "There was never any trouble at the Crossties before I started working here."

Alex's gaze shot to Joy's. He wanted to alleviate Mia's guilt, but he didn't know how. "*Have* you had trouble before?"

She shrugged, wiping at her eyes with her apron. "We had some fences broken. Cattle that got loose. But . . . nothing like this."

Alex's jaw locked. "Stay here with Joy, Mia." He glanced at Joy. "Do you have a weapon, Mrs. McCauley?"

She nodded, her hands knotted in her apron. "Henry's rifle."

"Do you know how to shoot?"

"No, I hate guns." Joy glanced up at him, fear pinching her face. "You think the killer will come here?"

Alex frowned. "I think he escaped in that vehicle I heard on the road. But we can't be too careful." He touched Mia's arms. "Can you shoot a rifle?"

"Yes," she said, her voice stronger now. "If anyone comes after Joy, I won't hesitate."

He hugged her to him. "Protect yourself, too, Mia. Remember that. Geoff is a sick bastard, and nothing he does or has done is your fault."

Her gaze met his, an agonized look that made him hate her ex all over again.

The son of a bitch deserved to die for what he'd put Mia through. And if he tried to hurt her again, Alex would kill him and not think twice.

GEOFF DROVE TO THE dump nearest the ranch, then took the scissors he'd picked up at Mia's and began slicing her underwear. Ugly plain cotton panties and bras that she should never have purchased.

What was wrong with her?

She'd traded all her nice designer dresses and shoes for rugged jeans and western shirts and boots. Clothes befitting a common worker, not his wife.

Had she already forgotten all he'd taught her about how to dress to appeal to him? About the satin and lace that he liked?

About the skin that he wanted exposed, so he could look at her, touch her, taste her?

He would have her soon. And this time it would last forever.

CHAPTER 7

Alex jumped back in the saddle and sent the bay into a sprint toward the dining hall. When he arrived, he noted several other horses tied outside along with Henry McCauley's black pickup and a Wrangler jeep.

He dismounted, then strode inside, wiping sweat from his brow. Henry met him at the door to the dining hall, his face ashen. "I can't believe this happened," he said in a broken voice. "Joleen was a good woman. She never hurt a soul."

Alex gritted his teeth. He didn't want the woman's death on Mia's shoulders. Not that he blamed Mia, but he understood the irrational guilt that could eat at a person and was afraid she'd blame herself.

God knows he'd felt it before. That first case, the young woman who'd died because he'd been too late.

He shut out the memory. He'd hated himself for a long

time. Just as he'd hated himself for letting the girl die in foster care.

But he was as stubborn as Mia and refused to give up. Because giving up meant the bad guys would win.

And that wasn't an option. Geoff Jones would pay for this.

"Who found her?" Alex asked Henry.

"My foreman, Drew Bates. He came over early. I asked him to meet us here and talk to you before you questioned my hands."

Henry gestured toward a gray-haired man with a paunch and a thick beard. In spite of his size, the man looked visibly shaken as Henry introduced the two of them.

"I understand you discovered her body, Mr. Bates," Alex said.

Bates mumbled a pained yeah. "I knew the minute I opened the door and didn't smell anything cooking in the chow hall that something was wrong."

"Joleen's a great cook." Henry's eyes clouded over. "Well, she was."

"Made the best country fried steak in Texas." Bates patted his belly. "I gained twenty pounds the first month she started cooking for us."

"When was that?" Alex asked.

The two men exchanged sad looks. "About five years ago," Henry answered. "Her husband used to work for me, but she lost him to cancer. Joleen and Joy have been friends for years. Joy thought Joleen needed something to do with her time. She loved cooking, so we asked her if she wanted the job."

Bates rubbed his chin. "Before we had her, this old guy named Wilbert used to cook. Everything tasted the same.

Burned the fried chicken ever damn time."

"Did Joleen have any enemies?" Alex asked.

Both men shook their hands. "She was sixty-two years old, a grandmother, cook, friend," Henry said.

"Everyone here loved her." Bates's voice cracked. "The young guys talked about her like she was their mama."

Alex grimaced. "Show me where she is."

Henry grimaced but led Alex through the dining hall then through a set of double doors to a small suite built in the back.

Alex immediately scanned the room, noting details. "Call the sheriff and tell him to bring a crime unit out here. We need to sweep for forensics."

Henry nodded and stood back while Alex slowly entered the room. Joleen was sprawled on the wood floor, her eyes wide in death, her jaw slack.

Blood coated the front of her blouse, soaking her shirt and lap. She must have tried to stop the bleeding with her hands, because they were covered in blood, and more blood streaked the wall where it appeared she'd tried to drag herself up from the floor to call for help. The phone lay off the cradle, a busy signal echoing in the silence.

He inched closer, knelt and felt her arm. Cold. Stiff. Rigor was setting in.

But her murder didn't make sense.

If Geoff had killed her, what was his motive? Joleen had posed no threat to him.

Had he held her hostage long enough to force her to tell him where Mia's cabin was then shot her to keep her from warning Mia he was coming?

"I know Geoff is dangerous," Mia said to Joy. "But I don't understand why he'd shoot Joleen."

Joy yanked more tissue from the box and wiped her eyes. "He must be a desperate man."

Mia nodded. She'd seen the news, knew some guards had been murdered, but for some reason, had assumed the other men committed the murders.

When they'd been together, Geoff had only vented his rage against her.

Prison had obviously changed him.

Mia paced the living room. "When Alex returns, I'll leave the Crossties."

"No, you won't. Besides, we don't know for certain your ex did this," Joy said, although her voice warbled.

"He was at my cabin," Mia said. "He left me flowers and a note." She refused to tell Joy about the underwear. It was too humiliating.

"I've heard about men stalking women," Joy said. "I suppose I was lucky all those years ago to find Henry."

"You were lucky and *smart*," Mia said, emphasizing the last word. "Geoff was my mistake. No one else should have to suffer for it." Maybe she should go on TV, make a plea for Geoff to meet her. Trade her life so he wouldn't hurt anyone else.

A siren wailed, and she looked out the window and saw the sheriff's car and a crime van pulling up.

Joy pushed to her feet. "I'll point them in the direction of the dining hall."

"No." Mia squeezed her shoulder. "Stay here and drink your tea. I'll tell them where to go."

Mia didn't wait for an argument. She stepped onto the front porch and waited until the men approached.

"Sheriff Leonard, Ma'am." He tipped his hat." Mr. McCauley called about a murder."

"Yes," Mia said. "He and Sgt. Townsend are at the dining hall." She gestured toward the turn a few feet away. "The cook Joleen Perry was shot." She inhaled a deep breath. "I think I know who did it."

The sheriff squinted through the fading sun. "Who would that be, Ma'am?"

"My ex-husband Geoff Jones. He's one of the escaped prisoners. He came here looking for me."

ALEX SNAPPED PHOTOS OF the crime scene with his cell phone. The gunshot wound, the way Joleen's body was lying on the floor, her hand reaching out for help . . .

Help that hadn't come in time.

There were no signs of a struggle though. Everything seemed neat and tidy as if the shooter had surprised her. The small suite was filled with kitty cat knick-knacks and Afghans she'd probably knitted herself. Pictures of three children along with a woman and man in their thirties sat on the kitchen counter.

A pang hit him. Her family would have to be called.

He walked around the body, then noticed a bullet casing beneath the table and snapped a photo of it. It looked like a slug from a .38.

The sound of an engine puttering echoed from outside, and he walked to the front to see the sheriff's car and crime unit roll up. Some of Henry's ranch hands had already arrived for dinner and their meeting, and Alex had asked Henry to keep the men outside and not to let anyone leave. He didn't want the crime scene contaminated, and all the men on the ranch had to be questioned.

Alex needed solid evidence to prove that Jones had murdered Joleen, too. Then he could add a homicide charge to his other charges. Combined with his previous sentence, Geoff wouldn't see daylight for a long damn time.

And any chance of his haughty parents denying that Geoff was a criminal would be lost forever.

They made quick introductions as the sheriff and crime team met him at the door.

"We spoke to Ms. Matthews," Sheriff Leonard said. "She thinks her ex-husband killed this woman."

Alex gritted his teeth. "It's possible. Jones is obsessed with Mia. We believe he came after her for revenge."

"I remember that trial. Don't have any use for wife beaters myself," Sheriff Leonard muttered sourly.

"Me neither," Alex said. "Jones has been on the ranch. He left flowers and a note on Mia's doorstep and messed with her clothing inside the house."

The sheriff studied Joleen's body where it lay on the floor in a pool of blood. "Why did he kill Joleen?"

"I don't know," Alex said. "Maybe he came here looking for Mia. Joleen could have recognized him from the news and tried to call the police."

The sheriff hooked his thumbs in his belt. "That makes sense."

Alex gestured toward the crime techs. "Sweep this place good, especially this room. The dining hall will have dozens of prints from the ranch hands." He looked up at the sheriff. "Maybe you can help me question the employees. We'll need their prints for comparison as well."

"Sure thing." Sheriff Leonard went to his car to retrieve his fingerprinting kit while the techs began combing the room for forensics.

Alex divided the list of employees between himself and the sheriff, then stepped outside to address the ranch hands. "Listen, guys, I know you're all wondering what's going on. Your cook Joleen was murdered. The sheriff and I need to talk to each of you. If you know anything about Joleen's murder, please tell us up front." He paused. "We'll also need your fingerprints for elimination purposes."

Several of the men shifted, looking nervous, and a rumble of low voices echoed protests. He sensed a couple of the men were illegal immigrants, and one or two had records.

"Listen, the sheriff and I are not interested in your papers if you're working on obtaining legal status. What we want is to find Joleen's killer."

Alex set up station on the right side of the dining hall while the sheriff took the left. Henry and Bates were put in charge of watching the door and keeping the men calm and under control.

The first three men Alex questioned had worked with Henry for over ten years, seemed completely devoted to Henry, boasted about what a great employer and friend he was. They all adored Joleen to the point of being visibly shaken and distraught. None of them argued about being fingerprinted either and all denied ever having been in Joleen's suite.

Dammit, he wished he'd had time to run background checks on all of them and look at their financials. If one of the hands needed money, Geoff could easily have used that weakness in his favor.

He carefully worded his questions to probe the subject.

"Listen to me," Barry Ernest said. "We don't make a fortune here, but it's steady money, enough to support our families."

"And we get housing," another hand told him.

Alex dismissed those three, then asked Truitt Wilson to join him alone at the table. Wilson seemed apprehensive and drummed his fist on the table.

"This is awful," he said, "Ms. Joleen reminded me of my grandma."

"Do you own a gun?" Alex asked.

Wilson fidgeted. "A shotgun. But you know, Sergeant, we need it when we're out working the cattle. Snakes and all."

True. "Hang on a minute." He put in a call to his chief and asked him to obtain a warrant to allow them to search the men's bunks and their personal belongings. If one of them had a .38, they'd have it tested to see if it was the murder weapon.

Alex consulted Wilson's file. "It says here that you're from Austin."

Wilson's eyes narrowed. "What does that have to do with anything?"

"Did you know a man named Geoff Jones?"

His fist tightened on the table. "I heard of him. He was that lawyer who went to jail for beating his wife."

"That's right," Alex said. "He almost killed her. Did you know him?"

"No," Wilson, said his tone becoming defensive. "Why? You think he murdered Ms. Joleen?"

Alex leaned forward, using his size and cold stare to intimidate the young man. "He escaped prison and came here looking for Mia. She's his ex-wife."

Wilson coughed, a panicked look twisting his face.

"We also believe that Jones hired someone to find her. How did you find out about the job here?"

Realization dawned, Truitt's eyes widening with fear. "I heard about it in town," he said. "But I'm not working for Jones if that's what you're implying."

Out of the corner of his eye, Alex saw something moving. A man.

He zeroed in on the man's face. His flat nose, wide jaw, the scar above his eyebrow. Emmett Ross. He recognized him from the employee file.

Emmett was sneaking out the back door.

"Stay here, I'm not done with you," Alex warned.

Alex raced after Emmett, but Emmett spotted him, darted out the back door and made a run for the woods.

MIA JUMPED AT THE SOUND of her cell phone ringing. Assuming it was Alex with news about Joleen, she snatched it from her purse without bothering to look at the caller ID screen.

"Hello, Alex—"

"No, it's me, Mia."

Nausea rose to her throat at the husky sound of Geoff's voice.

"No one will ever love you like I do."

A chill skated up Mia's spine.

"You don't know what love means," Mia snapped. "You're a monster."

"And you're my wife. A very naughty disobedient one, but you'll learn."

"I will never obey you," Mia whispered.

"You'd better." His voice turned low, more menacing. "If you don't, everyone around you will die."

CHAPTER 8

A LEX JOGGED OUTSIDE. "WAIT a minute, Royce."

Instead of stopping, the man picked up his pace, running toward the woods. Alex cursed and sprinted after him, grateful for his training as he caught the man and tackled him.

"Let go of me," Royce shouted. "I haven't done anything wrong."

Alex jerked his arm behind him, twisting it to a painful level. "Then why the hell were you running?"

Royce struggled slightly, and Alex tightened his hold. "Why. Were. You. Running?"

"Let me go and I'll talk."

Alex jerked him sideways and slammed him up against a tree. "Talk and *then* I might let you go."

A frustrated heave came from the wiry man, his nostrils flaring as he stared up at Alex. "Because I have a record. And I knew the minute you found out, you'd look at me as a suspect."

"Right now, everyone is a suspect," Alex said. "What was your prior for?"

Royce's lips thinned into a snarl. "Assault and battery."

Alex arched a brow. "Who did you assault?"

"A friend of mine. At least he used to be before he screwed my wife."

Alex studied him, then gave a nod of understanding. "Where did you do time?"

"The state pen," Royce said.

The hair on the back of Alex's neck prickled. "Do you know a man named Geoff Jones?"

Royce cut his eyes sideways. That hesitation gave Alex his answer.

"Let me rephrase that. Did he pay you to track down his ex-wife?"

Royce jerked his gaze back to him. "What the hell are you talking about? And what's this got to do with Ms. Joleen being murdered?"

"That's what I'm trying to figure out," Alex growled low in his throat. "Now, answer the damn question. Did he hire you to find his ex-wife?"

Royce shook his head, a vein pulsing in his neck. "No. Why would he?"

"Because he's obsessed with her and broke out of jail," Alex snapped. "And he's here on the ranch."

Royce's eyes widened, a seed of worry flickering in his expression. "His wife is *here*?"

"Don't act like you don't know what I'm talking about. Have you spoken to Jones or seen him lately?"

Royce looked down at Alex's hands where he was gripping Royce by the shirt. "No. I met him in the prison, but only because my cellmate knew him. I didn't like the bastard. The feeling was mutual." He angled his cheek so Alex could see his puckered scar. "He gave me that just because I dared challenge him."

"If you're lying, I'll find out," Alex said gruffly.

"I'm telling you the truth." Royce clenched his jaw. "You think he killed Ms. Joleen?"

Alex hesitated. "He's top on my suspect list."

"Then I hope you find the asshole," Royce muttered. "Ms. Joleen was like a mama to us guys here on the ranch."

The sincerity in the man's voice made Alex loosen his grip.

"Don't leave town," Alex said.

"I can't," Royce said bitterly. "I'm on parole."

Maybe the guy was trying to get back on his feet and telling the truth. Alex relaxed, but Royce arched his brows.

"You said you thought he paid someone to find his wife. Why would you think she's at the Crossties?"

"Because she is here," Alex said. "Mia Matthews used to be married to him."

Royce dropped his hands to his sides. "That explains a lot."

"What does that mean?"

"Why she's so standoffish to all the men here. Two or three of the hands asked her out, but she turned them down flat."

Alex's pulse hammered. "Were you one of them?"

Royce gave a self-deprecating laugh. "Yeah. But hell, now I'm glad she did. I heard Jones say he'd kill anyone who touched her."

———————

MIA'S INSTINCT WAS TO run as far away as she could.

Not only to protect herself but to protect those around her who she cared about.

If Joleen had died because of her, she would never forgive herself for coming to the Crossties.

"We're going to have to let Joleen's family know about her death," Joy said, her voice strained with emotions.

Mia's stomach clenched. "She has a daughter?"

"Yes, she lives in Houston with her husband and three children. She'll be devastated."

More guilt heaped onto the pile.

"I'm so sorry, Joy. Sorry for Joleen and her family and . . . sorry for coming here."

Joy brushed her hands down her apron then pulled Mia into a hug. "This is absolutely not your fault," Joy said firmly.

Mia hugged the woman, but Joy's reassuring words fell on deaf ears.

How could it not be her fault if Geoff had killed Joleen because of her?

A noise sounded outside, and Joy looked up, stricken. "What was that?"

Dusk had set, the sun already faded so night shadows plagued the land as Mia glanced out the window. A dozen different scenarios taunted her.

Geoff had called her only a few minutes ago. Was he in the woods watching now?

Perhaps sneaking up to the house to trap her while Alex and the other men were at the dining hall?

Had he killed Joleen to lure Alex away from her so he could gain easier access to her?

She grabbed the rifle and braced it by her side. "Stay here, Joy, I'll be right back."

If Geoff showed up, she'd be ready.

Suddenly a window crashed in the living room.

Mia raced to the hallway and screamed at Joy to run out the back just as smoke began to fill the room.

By the time Alex went back inside the dining hall, the ME was there.

"What happened?" Sheriff Leonard asked.

"Emmett Royce tried to run. I caught him."

Henry rubbed at his chin. "Did Royce hurt Joleen?"

"I don't think so," Alex said. "But he was in prison with Geoff Jones. He claims he hated the man though and has a scar to prove they weren't friends."

"Do you believe him?" Sheriff Leonard asked.

Alex shrugged. "I think so. Did you learn anything from the other hands?"

Sheriff Leonard gestured toward a thin, dirty-blond haired guy dusty from working the ranch. "Troy Durgin over there said he thought he saw someone in the woods behind the dining hall earlier. Fits with the time of death."

"Which was?" Alex asked.

"Shortly after lunch."

So, everyone had cleared out of the dining hall except Joleen. The shooter would have known she was alone and that no one would show up until dinnertime.

She'd been vulnerable. If she'd tried to call for help, Jones would have killed her to keep his presence unknown.

Sick fucks like him took pleasure in tormenting their victims. Playing with them. Enjoying their fear.

Alex walked over to the lead crime tech, and the ME and introduced himself.

"What can you tell us from the body, Doc?"

Dr. Cato pointed to Joleen's bloody chest. "She died of a single gunshot wound that pierced her heart. No other visible injuries."

Alex frowned. "No bruises or rope marks to suggest that she was coerced?"

Cato shook his head. "I'd say the shooter surprised her with the gun. She probably thought if she cooperated, he'd spare her."

"Any sign of robbery?" Alex asked on the off chance that her murder wasn't connected to Jones. Robberies turned into murder all the time.

Lt. Ponderson from the CSU team spoke up, "It didn't appear that anything was missing. Her ID, wallet with a hundred dollars in cash, was still intact. She was still wearing a gold cross and wedding band."

"Even if her jewelry wasn't worth much, a robber would have at least taken the cash," Alex said.

"So, we think one of the workers on the ranch killed the woman?" Lt. Ponderson asked.

"Either that or someone who snuck on the ranch did," Alex said. "We're questioning each of the employees. Now we know the time of death, we can check alibis."

"But you have another theory?" Dr. Cato asked.

Alex explained Mia's situation and Jones's prison escape.

Henry ran toward them, his breath ragged. "There's smoke at the house! I gotta go."

"Smoke?" Panic seized Alex, and he turned to the sheriff. "I have to go, too. Mia's there. Question the rest of the man, and don't let anyone leave until you get his alibi for the time of death." He glanced at the ME and Lt. Ponderson. "Call me if you lift any prints, DNA or other forensic evidence."

He palmed his gun as he followed Henry outside to his truck. They jumped in and Henry pressed the gas, his craggy face terrified as they bounced over the ruts in the dirt drive leading back toward the farmhouse.

Smoke curled upward in a thick cloud from the front room, flames sparking through the window in the distance. Three more minutes and they would be there.

But fire could spread quickly, especially in an old wooden home.

"Call the fire department!" Henry shouted.

Alex punched in the emergency number, praying that Mia and Joy were all right.

THE SMOKE WAS SO thick Mia couldn't see. She shouted for Joy, but she didn't hear her respond. Where was she?

Frantic, she plowed through the den back toward the kitchen, hoping the woman had escaped. But Joy was nowhere to be seen.

Mentally she debated on whether to call for help before the fire spread or to find her.

Joy. She had to make sure her friend was safe and alive.

She screamed her name again, smoke already filling the kitchen and starting to fog her vision. She stumbled forward, ran into the table and winced.

"Joy?"

A low groan echoed from her right, and she spun toward the sound, her lungs straining for air.

Joy. Dear God. She was lying in a heap on the floor half unconscious.

Mia darted toward her, knelt and stroked Joy's cheek. "Come on, we have to get out of here. The living room is on fire."

Joy moaned, and Mia saw blood trickling down her forehead.

Someone had hit Joy over the head. Had Geoff tried to kill her as he had Joleen?

She gently shook Joy, but she didn't budge. "Come on, we have to get out of here." But Joy had passed out again.

Mia tried to lift her, but she was too heavy. Her lungs straining for air, she slid her arms beneath Joy's arms and dragged her toward the back door.

"I'm sorry, so sorry," Mia whispered. She kicked the door open with her foot and pulled Joy the rest of the way outside then onto the ground a few feet away beneath a Blackgum tree.

A second later, a car engine rumbled down the drive, but it was hard to tell who it was over the sound of the fire crackling.

She bent and hugged Joy. "I'll be back with help. Hang in there, Joy."

She turned to run around the front of the house, hoping to see Alex or the sheriff, but suddenly something slammed into the back of her head.

Mia cried out, stumbled, then hit the ground, and the world went black.

CHAPTER 9

As soon as Henry braked, Alex hit the ground running. He didn't wait until the truck had stopped. Seconds later, he heard the engine die and Henry's labored breathing behind him as the older man jogged after Alex.

One look at the front of the house though, and Alex noted the flames eating the living room curtains. He gestured toward Henry. "Around back. We can't go in the front."

Alex darted left, calling Mia's name as he glanced through the side windows. Smoke was creeping in the hallway toward the back. "Mia!" he shouted again.

Please God, let her be okay.

The sound of fire crackling popped into the night, a breeze stirring, making the situation more dangerous with every second. The fire would spread to the dry grass outside if they didn't contain it soon. He made it to the back steps, scanning left and right, then spotted Joy slumped onto the ground beneath a tree unconscious.

"Henry, there's Joy!" He ran toward her, knelt and checked her pulse. Low and thready, but she was alive. "Call an ambulance," he said as Henry lumbered up.

The poor man looked panic-stricken and was sweating as he dropped to his knees and dragged his wife into his arms.

"Baby, hang in there, it'll be all right."

Alex gave Henry's shoulders a gentle shake then shoved his cell phone into Henry's hands. "Henry, call an ambulance. I have to find Mia."

The older man seemed to jerk himself out of his shock, took the phone and started punching in numbers.

Alex raced up the steps to the front porch, heat and smoke suffusing him as he ran through the open back door. "Mia!" The smoke was so thick he could barely see, but the kitchen was empty.

Had Mia dragged Joy to safety? If so, why wasn't she outside with her?

"Mia!" He stepped into the hallway, scanning the living room that was being eaten by the flames, and squinted through the blaze in search of Mia. But he didn't see or hear anyone inside.

The steps were to the left, so he jogged up them, dodging a patch of fire on the bottom step. He had to hurry before it spread. Already, smoke was rising, thick and suffocating toward the bedrooms.

"Mia!" No sound.

Why would she have gone upstairs? Unless she'd been up

there when it started, and Joy had gotten herself out. But once the smoke curled upward, Mia would have come downstairs.

Unless she was hurt and unable to.

Pure fear paralyzed him for a moment. What if Jones had knocked Mia unconscious and left her in the house to die?

Fire crackled and a board splintered down, dragging him from his terror. He had to hurry. Every second counted.

He took the steps two at a time, then checked the first bedroom and adjoining bath. Empty. Covering his mouth with a handkerchief to keep from inhaling more smoke, he ran to the next bedroom, then the master suite.

Both empty.

Panicking, he jogged back down the steps, jumping over patches of flames and the burning rug. A siren wailed, coming closer.

The fire truck. Maybe the ambulance was close behind.

But where in the hell was Mia?

MIA ROUSED FROM UNCONSCIOUSNESS and realized someone was carrying her through the woods.

Geoff?

He had thrown her over his shoulder, the sickening smell of sweat hitting her. "Let me go!" She screamed and clawed at his back, struggling to make him put her down.

His hands tightened on her backside, another hand pressing firmly against her legs where she was kicking at him. She beat at his back with her fists, then yanked at his hair.

It was long and shaggy.

Not Geoff.

"Let me go!" she cried again.

"Shut the fuck up," the man hissed.

Anger mingled with pure fear, and Mia suddenly sank her teeth into his shoulder. She bit down hard, biting him with all her might.

He bellowed, yanked her head up by her hair then threw her down, sending her sprawling into a cluster of trees. The backs of her legs hit a stump, weeds clawing at her legs and arms, the sound of twigs and bramble breaking.

"You stupid bitch!" the man snarled.

Mia frantically searched the ground for a weapon. Her hand came up with a stick, and she grabbed it, using it like a sword as he lunged toward her. She managed to jab him in the stomach once, then he caught her by the waist. Remembering the self-defense classes she'd taken, she jabbed him in the eyes with her fingers.

He yelled and cursed, drawing back, temporarily disoriented with the pain. But she quickly recovered. She had to get away.

Pushing to her feet, she ran back toward the ranch.

A loud curse echoed behind her, and sticks and leaves crunched as he raced after her. The world spun, her vision blurring as she wove between the trees. She stumbled over a limb and nearly fell but caught herself and trudged on.

The smoke from the house curled into the sky, the flames drawing her eyes.

"You're going to pay for biting me!" the man yelled.

"Help!" she cried as a branch slapped her in the face. "Someone help!"

He was getting closer, gaining on her. She could hear his breathing. Smell the sweat pouring off of him.

The house loomed so far away. She felt his fingers snatching at her back. Catching in her hair.

She ran faster. If he caught her this time, she might not get away.

THE AMBULANCE ROARED UP just as Alex ran out the back of the house again. The fire truck had arrived, and firefighters were already rolling out the hoses and spraying water on the flames.

Two medics knelt by Joy, examining her.

Alex's heart hammered. Mia wasn't in the house. What if Geoff had her?

In spite of the heat from the fire, cold fear swept over him. He'd promised to protect her, and he'd failed.

The noise of the water spraying rent the air, but suddenly he froze. He thought he heard a scream

He pivoted, scanning the property. The silhouette of a person moving in the woods caught his eye.

Another scream.

Mia.

She was running, but a man was chasing her, close on her tail.

Yanking his gun from his holster, he darted in the direction of the figure. His lungs strained for air as he jogged into the thicket of trees. With daylight long gone and only a sliver of the moon to illuminate the woods, he lost Mia for a moment.

Terror overwhelmed him. Geoff must have orchestrated the fire to lure Mia outside. Killing Joleen had been a diversion.

Another scream pierced the air, and he cursed and picked up his pace, dashing to the right and jumping over branches that must have been blown down in a storm.

The sound of a man's snarl made his stomach clench, and he spotted a hulking figure lunge at Mia. She went down, the man on top of her.

Pure rage assaulted Alex, and he tightened his grip on his gun and hurled himself through the weeds. A few feet more and he saw the man drag Mia up by the hair.

She was panting and fighting, kicking back at him, fighting like a wildcat.

Alex inched behind a tree, raised his gun and aimed it at the man's head. "Let her go or you're dead."

Leaves rustled as the man's head whipped to the left toward him. Alex sized him up quickly.

Not Geoff. This man was larger, burly, had a beard, and hands the size of ham hocks.

Alex's finger tightened on the trigger. "I said let her go. Now."

"Son of a bitch," the man snarled.

Mia's shaky breathing rattled in the silence as Alex stepped from behind the tree to reveal himself and his weapon, which he kept trained on the man's head.

"I'm not going to say it again," Alex said. "Release her this second or take a bullet."

The man dropped his hands from Mia's hair. She stumbled, caught herself against a tree and shoved strands of her hair from her face. Blood trickled down her forehead, sending his temper to a boiling high.

"Are you all right, Mia?"

Her gaze met his, her eyes filled with fear. But he recognized fight there as well. "Yes."

But she wasn't all right and they both knew it. She'd obviously sustained a blow to the head, and no telling what else. She'd been missing less than half an hour but a lot could happen in that time.

His gaze skated over her, assessing. At least her clothes were intact.

The bastard who'd attacked her shifted and Alex shook his head in warning. If the jerk touched her again, Alex would kill him with his bare hands.

"Go ahead. Try to run," he said in a menacing voice. "Give me a reason to blow your head off."

The man's hands flew upward in surrender. "No. Don't shoot."

"Who are you?" Alex asked.

Sweat poured down the man's ruddy skin. "Look, I wasn't going to hurt her, but the bitch bit me."

Alex slid his hand into his pocket and removed a pair of handcuffs, then quickly yanked the guy's hands behind his back and snapped the cuffs tight. "I asked you your name."

"Fuck you."

Alex ground his teeth. "Why did you abduct Mia?"

The man's jowls puffed out, and he glanced at Mia. Her

breathing was finally steadying, but she was still trembling. He wanted to drag her in his arms and hold her, comfort her.

Alleviate her fear.

Kill the man who'd hurt her.

Alex twisted the man around and flung him up against a tree so hard the man winced in pain.

Alex raised his gun and pointed it straight at his eyes. "Tell me."

"I—"

But the bastard never got to finish the sentence. A bullet whizzed by Alex's head and penetrated the jerk's skull. The man's eyes widened just as the bullet entered, then he dropped to the ground, blood and brains splattering across the dirt.

Mia screamed, and he lunged toward her, pulled her in his arms and yanked her safely behind a smattering of trees in case the shooter fired again.

CHAPTER 10

Mia clutched Alex's arms as he dragged her to the ground to cover her. He checked her for injuries, but she brushed away his hands and his concern. She couldn't take her eyes off the man who'd been shot.

Blood gushed from his head, the top of his skull exposed, his body limps. He'd been shot right in front of her eyes.

"Mia, are you okay?" Alex asked gruffly.

She nodded, shock straining her features.

"Do you know who he was?" Alex asked.

She shook her head no. "Joy and I were in the kitchen, and I heard the window crash. When I went into the living room, I saw the smoke and yelled at Joy to run out the back."

Alex cradled her face between his hands. "Did you see Geoff?"

"No," she said shakily. "When I ran back to the kitchen, Joy was on the floor. I helped her outside, then was going to call for help, but someone hit me over the back of the head."

She automatically touched the spot where she'd been hit, sticky blood coating her fingertips and matting her hair.

Alex craned his head to look for the shooter. For all they knew, the son of a bitch could have a half dozen hired men working for him. All ready to snatch Mia at his beck and call. "What happened then?"

"When I came to, that man was dragging me through the woods."

"Was Geoff a good marksman?" Alex asked.

"Not when I knew him. But he had to be good to have hit that man from a distance." She looked up at him, her eyes haunted. "Or do you think Geoff was shooting at *me*?"

"No, I think the shooter wanted to abduct you and take you to Jones."

Because Geoff wouldn't kill Mia, at least not at first.

He was just the type of sadistic monster who'd toy with her. Torment her. Make her suffer.

A sound cut through the tense silence, branches and twigs snapping, and a figure sprinted up the hill toward the west end near the road.

Alex cursed.

Mia nudged his shoulder. "Go after him."

"I'm not leaving you." Alex pulled her up against him. "I made that mistake before. Not again."

Alex hugged her to him, punching in a number on his phone. "Sheriff, this is Sgt. Townsend. A man tried to kidnap Mia. I caught up with them, but a shooter was in the woods and killed Mia's attacker. We'll need the crime techs and the ME here to examine his body and transport him to the morgue."

"Jesus, what a cluster," the sheriff said. "First Joleen, then the fire and now this."

"It has to all be related," Alex said. "Killing Joleen was a diversion, then the fire was set to draw Mia out. She took a blow to the head."

"This is some determined fucker," Sheriff Leonard muttered. "I'll send one of the techs and Dr. Ponderson over there."

"Good. I'll wait here until one of you arrives." Even if the dead man couldn't talk, identifying him could help solve the case.

If he'd murdered Joleen, her family deserved to know and have closure as they laid her to rest.

———————

MIA SANK DOWN ONTO the ground and leaned against the tree, her head spinning. She couldn't believe all this was happening. Twenty-four hours ago, she'd thought she was safe. She'd been happy riding across the ranch.

Now Joleen had been injured, the farmhouse might be lost, and another man was dead.

All because of her.

"This has to stop, Alex."

Alex knelt beside her and squeezed her hands between his. "We will stop it, Mia. Just hang in there, okay?"

She nodded numbly, although she desperately wanted to turn back the clock. Leave the Crossties before anyone else she cared about was hurt.

The McCauleys were the closest thing to family she'd ever known. She hated that they'd been drawn into her problems with her sick, twisted ex.

Alex walked over to the man's body, dug into the pocket of his jeans and pulled out a wallet. He flipped it open and checked the ID. "Man's name is Farr Olander. Do you recognize the name?"

"I've never seen or heard of him," Mia said, averting her eyes from the gruesome bloody scene. Although she had a feeling she'd be seeing his shattered head in her nightmares for years.

The sound of a car screeching up to the house echoed from the dirt road down the hill, and minutes later the sheriff and ME approached them.

Smoke still curled in the sky above the house, but she didn't see flames anymore. Hopefully, the firefighters had contained the blaze before it could spread through the house. But there would be smoke and water damage.

The sheriff ambled up, eyes narrowed as he spotted the dead man on the ground. "Well, this is a helluva day. Who is he?"

"His name is Farr Olander." Alex handed the sheriff the man's wallet. "He probably works for Jones, but let's verify that and find out everything we can about him."

A crime tech strode toward them, and Alex explained what had happened.

"I'm going to make sure the medics examine Mia while you guys handle transporting his body to the morgue."

"You shot him?" the sheriff asked.

Alex shook his head. "No, the shooter was up there in the

woods. He got away. Look for bullet casings. Maybe we can match them to the gun that killed Joleen and connect the dots."

Mia's heart ached as she thought of Joleen. Joleen's daughter and grandchildren would be devastated when they heard she was gone.

Alex returned to her side, held out his hand and helped her to stand. "Come on, Mia. You need to get checked out."

"I'm fine," Mia said although she felt shaky from the ordeal, relented and allowed herself to lean on Alex as they walked down the hill back to the house. The scent of charred wood suffused the air, but at least the house was still standing.

It looked as if the firefighters had contained the blaze to the front of the house, but there still was extensive damage.

Poor Joy and Henry. She'd have to figure out a way to pay for the repairs.

As soon as she saw Joy on the stretcher beside the ambulance, she let go of Alex and ran toward her. Regret mingled with relief.

At least Joy was alive. But she never would have been hurt if not for Mia.

Henry hovered beside his wife, his face ashen with fear for Joy.

Mia stopped by the stretcher and looked down at her friend. "Joy, I'm so sorry. Are you okay?"

"Yes, honey, are you?" Joy ran her fingers over Mia's face.

"Yes. But I'm so sorry, Joy. You're hurt, and your house is damaged . . . I'll try to pay you back . . ."

Anger and sorrow surged through Mia. The McCauleys didn't deserve this.

"Our house is just a house," Joy said. "You are far more important, dear," Joy whispered.

Tears blurred Mia's eyes, and she looked up at Henry, expecting to see anger, but compassion and love shimmered in his expression.

Henry wiped at his teary eyes. "She's right, as long as you girls are okay, everything else can be replaced."

"What happened?" Joy asked.

Alex had come up behind Mia, anger radiating from him. "There were two men," Alex said. "We think they were working for Jones, and that they set the fire to lure Mia outside."

He paused. "The man who attacked Mia was named Farr Olander. I caught him, but someone else in the woods shot him before I could bring him in. The shooter escaped."

"This is crazy," Mia said. "I can't go on like this."

"It's going to be all right," Alex said in a deep voice. "We'll find him, Mia."

Mia shook her head. "Let me go on TV. I'll make a plea with Geoff, agree to meet him if he'll leave everyone else I care about alone."

Joy and Henry both shook their heads in protest, eyes alarmed. "No, Mia," Joy said.

"We can't let you do that," Henry said at the same time.

Mia turned to Alex. "Please, Alex. I can't live with myself if anyone else is hurt because of me."

———————

THERE WAS NO WAY Alex would let Mia put herself in danger. No damn way.

But she was reacting in shock and running on emotions, guilt topping the list along with fear.

He summoned a low, calming voice. "We'll talk about a plan later. Right now, the paramedics need to examine you."

"I told you I'm fine," Mia protested.

"Humor me," Alex said softly.

Her gaze met his, a dozen feelings warring in her eyes. He hated her ex more than ever. How dare Jones say he loves her and torment her like this.

The bastard deserved to die.

He glanced at Henry and Joy. "You two okay?"

The couple clasped hands and nodded. "We will be," Henry said. "Now I know my Joy is safe."

"They want me to go to the hospital overnight for observation," Joy said.

Henry's brows furrowed with worry. "I'll be there with her all night." He leaned toward Alex. "You take care of Mia."

"Don't worry, I intend to," Alex said, hating the icy terror that gripped him at the thought of Jones touching her again. "I'll assign a guard to your property tonight."

Henry thanked him, and Alex conferred with the ME while the medics tended to the cut on the back of Mia's head.

"We're transporting Olander to the morgue. The sheriff will notify his family, if he has any." Dr. Ponderson frowned. "I just talked to the CSU team. They're ready to release Joleen as well."

Alex stepped aside and called the lieutenant. "Call me once you compare bullet casings, and on any forensics you find. I want someone combing the woods for the shooter and any evidence he left behind."

The man agreed, and Alex straightened as the fire chief approached. "The fire's contained, but it was definitely arson."

Alex gestured toward Mia. "Mia said someone tossed an object through the window right before the fire started. If you can find whatever that was and lift prints, it would help."

"We'll sort through the ashes once things cool, and I'll let you know what we find."

"Thanks."

Alex called the sheriff who'd remained with Olander's body and asked him to send a deputy out to the Crossties for the night. He didn't want any more damage done to the McCauley home than had already been done.

The fire investigator turned to Henry and explained about the arson. Alex was amazed at how calmly the older man handled the situation. But he obviously loved his wife and had his priorities in order.

Which made Alex think about Mia and how he'd always put work first.

Dammit to hell. He cared about her. He had from the minute he'd met her. He'd admired her guts in standing up to her bully of an ex and taking him to court.

And if he admitted the truth to himself, he'd wanted her a year ago when he'd met her.

He wanted her even more now.

But he wanted to comfort her, to hold her and keep her safe, even more than he wanted to make love to her.

To show her that not every man was brutal and possessive

and twisted like Geoff Jones.

The medics were finishing with her by the time he made it back to the ambulance. "Are you taking her in for observation, too?" he asked the paramedic.

The medic shook his head. "No, she refuses to go. She claims she's all right."

"Her vitals are normal, especially for what she's been through," the other medic said. "The cut on her head wasn't deep. She has some bruises, but no broken bones or signs of internal injuries."

Alex studied Mia, knowing she'd fake being well to avoid anyone hovering over her. "How about a concussion?"

"I am okay," Mia said, cutting off the conversation. "Now let them take Joy to the hospital."

Alex knew she was far from okay. But he didn't argue.

He wanted to take her away from the place as soon as he could, back to his cabin where he could make sure Jones couldn't get his hands on her tonight.

"GODDAMMIT! WHAT WAS THAT agent doing hovering so close to Mia? Was he fucking her?" Geoff squinted through the binoculars, every fiber of his body on alert just as it had been when he'd been locked in that infernal cell and he'd lain awake worried some asshole was going to try to kill him—or screw him—in the night.

He'd had to make friends fast. Exert his power. Find protection.

Those friends had served him well during his incarceration and had aided in his escape. They were loyal followers who would receive their payoff in the end.

As would Mia and that agent who had attached himself to her like a second skin.

His hand itched to pull the trigger again, and this time put the bullet between Sgt. Townsend's eyes. Blow his brains out and let Mia see how pretty the asswipe looked when he was dead.

But there were too many people around. Medics, the sheriff, deputies, crime scene techs.

No, he had to be patient.

Another skill prison had taught him.

Shooting Townsend right now would bring a dozen men breathing down his neck before he could escape.

He'd wait for the perfect moment. Lure the man away and make him sweat.

Make Mia suffer for even looking at the Ranger twice.

Then he'd kill him and force her to watch before he made her his again.

CHAPTER 11

Exhaustion pulled at Mia as she and Alex returned to her cabin.

"Pack a bag, Mia. You're not staying here tonight."

Mia planted her hands on her hips. "I won't allow him to run me off, Alex."

"Be reasonable, Mia. He'll do anything to get you. You need rest, and I doubt either one of us will sleep well here."

"But if he breaks in, you can catch him."

"No." A muscle ticked in Alex's strong jaw. "Putting yourself in danger will only reward him." He touched her arms, his eyes beseeching her. "Trust me. We'll find him but offering you up is not an option."

Emotions clogged Mia's throat. She hadn't trusted anyone since her disastrous marriage, not even herself.

But she did trust Alex.

He might be big and tough, gruff even, but he was an honorable man. He used his power and strength to save and protect others, not to force women to do his bidding.

She conceded with a weary sigh. "All right, give me a minute."

Mia ducked into the closet, removed an overnight bag, tossed in a pair of jeans and a long-sleeved white t-shirt for the next day, then went to her lingerie drawer.

The lacy underwear that Geoff had left for her mocked her, and she began to shake.

She slammed the drawer. She refused to wear anything that vile man had chosen for her. Instead, she'd ask Alex to stop at a discount store and she'd purchase some new underwear herself.

Something practical and sensible.

Except for a brief second, she glanced at Alex and wondered what he'd like her to wear.

Don't go there, Mia. He's protecting you because it's his job.

Frustration knotting her shoulders, she rushed to the bathroom and packed her toiletries, then decided to toss in an extra shirt and her denim jacket along with her pjs—boxers with a tank top.

Nothing that would look provocative or like she was trying to seduce Alex.

Seduce Alex...the thought held more appeal than she would ever have imagined. After being with Geoff, she never thought she'd want another man to touch her, much less make love to her.

And she'd certainly never imagined trusting a man.

"Are you ready?" Alex asked, his intense gaze raking over her as she joined him in the den.

She nodded, then remembered the revolver she'd bought and added it to her purse. If Geoff came for her or tried to hurt Alex, she'd shoot him without blinking an eye.

Alex didn't comment when she slipped it into her purse.

He placed his hand at the small of her back as they left the cabin, offering her comfort and confidence even though he perused the property in case of an attack.

On edge, Mia glanced down the road at the farmhouse as they drove away. The scent of smoke lingered in the air, reminding her of the earlier violence, of Joleen's death, and that Joy was in the hospital.

All because of her.

Hell, she hoped Geoff did come after her. She'd kill him for hurting her friends and for murdering Joleen.

ALEX SAW THE TURMOIL in Mia's eyes and knew she was blaming herself for what had happened tonight.

A dangerous mindset that could make her more vulnerable.

There was no way on God's green Earth he would let her offer herself as bait to catch her ex. The man should be rotting in jail for what he'd done.

And he would go back there soon.

Or to his grave.

Prison would be more painful, but as long as he was alive, Alex had no doubt he'd come back for Mia. Time and time again.

Death was the only way to stop him.

Adrenaline pumped through Alex. If he had to kill him, he would. He'd do anything to keep Mia safe.

Mia turned to look out the window at the smoke and charred front of the farmhouse as they passed, and Alex scanned the perimeter to make sure the deputy was still guarding the place. Not that he expected Jones to return tonight.

The man was too smart and knew when to retreat.

He—or his hired goons—had achieved their purpose by driving Mia from the house into Olander's clutches. But in doing so, they'd already drawn too much attention to themselves for one night.

Although Geoff still hadn't gotten what he'd wanted. Mia.

By God, he wouldn't either.

Not as long as Alex had a breath left in him.

He flipped on the radio to find some music, hoping to soothe Mia, but a special bulletin about the prison escape was airing.

"All three prisoners are to be considered armed and dangerous," the newscaster said. "Women in the area need to be especially cautious. Robert Simpleton was a serial killer and targeted brunettes in the Austin area."

Mia tensed, and Alex flipped the radio off, allowing the silence to fill the air. The last thing Mia needed was to hear more details about the prison escape. Even worse, she fit the profile of Simpleton's victims.

A cold knot of fear gripped him at the thought of her being hurt, and he sped up, veered onto the main highway and hightailed it toward his place. But just as he made it onto the highway, a dark sedan raced up behind him.

Alex heard the engine accelerate then headlights blinded him. He pressed the gas, wondering if the driver was drunk or if he was the shooter from the woods.

The driver increased his speed, closing the distance, and Alex glanced in the rearview mirror, straining to see the driver's face. But the windows were tinted, the headlights so bright that he couldn't make out a damn thing.

Suddenly the sedan sped up and rammed into them.

Mia cried out and gave him a panicked look. He jerked the wheel to try to maintain control, but his tires screeched, and the ditch loomed in front of them only inches away.

The driver rammed them again, sending his vehicle into a spin, then suddenly the car raced up beside him and a gunshot rang out.

He pushed Mia down. "Stay low!"

She ducked her head into his lap, and he yanked his gun from his holster and fired back just as the car shot past. His SUV spun out of control, and he had to force himself not to fight the spin or they'd roll.

The other car screeched ahead, did a one-eighty, then the driver gunned the engine and roared straight toward them. Mia glanced up and screamed.

Alex cursed, swung his weapon outside his window and fired at the sedan. The sedan swerved to avoid the bullet, and he fired another round. Glass exploded, and the vehicle skidded toward the embankment.

It spun in circles, then flipped, metal screeching as it slid across the road and careened into the ravine.

"Alex!" Mia cried.

He yanked the SUV to the right, his breathing rasping out as he wrangled for control. Finally, the brakes kicked in and he spun to a stop. He cut the engine, keeping his eyes trained on the embankment in case the driver surfaced.

"Stay here." Alex shoved her purse toward her. "And get that revolver out. If anyone approaches, shoot."

Fear streaked her face, but she nodded and caught his arm. "Be careful, Alex."

Touched by the concern in her voice, he gave her a quick nod, then pitched her his cell phone. "Call the sheriff and tell him what happened."

Chest heaving with adrenaline, he gripped his gun, climbed from his SUV and strode toward the ditch, casting his eyes in all directions in the case the driver had escaped and tried to sneak up on them.

Another car whizzed by, and he waited until it passed, then inched across the highway to the edge of the road. The sedan had crashed upside down into the ravine. From his vantage point, it appeared that the doors were still closed.

Rocks and dirt skittered below his feet as he descended the bank. He held his gun at the ready, searching around the vehicle in case the driver had escaped.

The scent of gasoline hit him, and his heart pounded. Was the gas tank going to blow?

He eased toward the car, carefully watching for the driver, but as he stepped closer, everything seemed still. Quiet. Eerily quiet.

He knelt, gun aimed at the window, and looked through the broken glass of the driver's window.

The driver was slumped over the steering wheel, blood covering the steering column. Alex reached in with one hand and yanked the man's head back, breathing easier when he realized the driver was dead.

But it wasn't Jones.

Hell, he wished the dead man was Jones. How many hired guns did the bastard have working for him?

The sudden thought that this man might have also a partner sent him running up the hill. He ran to the SUV and expelled a relieved breath when he saw Mia still inside.

Sirens wailed, and the sheriff's patrol car raced up. Alex waved him down. The sheriff's face was agitated as he climbed from his car.

"The driver's dead," Alex explained about the vehicle trying to run them off the road. The bullet holes puncturing the side of his car and shattered glass confirmed his story.

"This is unbelievable," the sheriff said. "Joleen's murder, the fire, an attack against Mia, a dead man, and now this."

"I told you Jones was one dangerous son of a bitch," Alex muttered.

"Take Mia someplace safe," the sheriff said. "I'll make sure the CSU identifies the driver and we'll process the scene."

Alex thanked him, dug one of the bullets from his SUV, put it in an evidence bag, and then handed it to the sheriff.

Then he crawled back in the car with Mia.

"What happened?" Mia asked.

He pressed a hand over hers. "The driver's dead."

"Was it Geoff?" she asked in a trembling voice.

"No, but we'll find out who he is."

Mia leaned back and closed her eyes, her breath a ragged whisper.

He started the engine then drove to his house, a rustic log cabin on the edge of a creek. He had a security system in place and an arsenal of weapons to choose from if Jones attacked.

MIA SHUDDERED, WRAPPING HER arms around herself to keep from falling apart as Alex drove. She felt numb, guilty, afraid.

Angry.

God help her.

She wanted Alex to hold her in his arms where she'd be safe.

But rational thoughts urged her to run so *he* would be safe.

Seconds ticked by, tension mounting inside her as they passed another ranch and more farmland, then Alex veered onto a dirt road about a half an hour from town.

"Where are we going?" she asked.

"To my cabin," Alex said. "Hopefully Jones won't look for you there. And if he does show up, I have a state-of-the-art security system."

She briefly wondered what kind of place the rugged cowboy lived in, then smiled for the first time in days when she spotted the rustic log cabin perched in the woods with the creek rippling in back.

"This is beautiful," she said softly as he parked in his garage.

Alex shrugged, a sheepish look on his face. "It's not fancy."

"I had fancy," Mia said. "I much prefer country. That's why I chose the ranch."

His eyes warmed, a small smile tilting his mouth as if her comment pleased him, then he climbed out and came around to help her. Mia was already pulling herself from the car, although her muscles ached, and her head was throbbing.

Alex retrieved her bag from the trunk of the SUV, took her arm and led her up the porch steps. A rocking chair and porch swing dominated the front porch, gorgeous giant trees engulfing the cabin, the scent of fresh air and something sweet, maybe honeysuckle, scenting the air.

He unlocked the door, then rushed to turn off the security system, while she stood in the entry admiring the wood floors, the stone fireplace that ran from the floor to ceiling, and the paintings of landscapes and horses that decorated the walls.

"Would you like to get a shower?" he asked.

Mia nodded. "Please." She needed the stench of that man's hands and his sweat off of her. Needed to forget that he'd dragged her through the woods and that if it wasn't for Alex, she'd be in Geoff's clutches now.

Or worse. Dead.

Then again, death would be preferable than being with Geoff.

Alex showed her to a guest room and bath with plush towels and a claw foot tub. The bedroom was homey but elegant with a handmade quilt covering a four-poster pine bed and an antique armoire in the corner.

"This is beautiful," she said again.

He shrugged. "I'm a simple man. I like simple things."

Alex was anything but simple. He never talked about himself; he only took care of others. Put his life on the line every day for strangers just as he'd done for her.

And he was all man—rugged, no-nonsense, muscular, a cowboy, and . . . the sexiest man she'd ever met.

Her stomach fluttered with nerves, desire heating her insides. But she glanced down at her disheveled clothing, felt the blood drying in her hair and dashed into the bathroom.

What man would want her?

Other than a sick one like Geoff . . .

Seconds later, she slipped into a warm bubble bath and relaxed, desperate to shove thoughts of Geoff and murder and his sick twisted ways from her mind.

Instead, she imagined Alex sinking into the tub with her, and her body tingled with need.

She wanted to be with him tonight. To crawl in his bed and feel his warm arms embracing her, to feel his breath on her body, to have him make her feel alive.

ALEX QUICKLY SHOWERED WHILE Mia soaked in the tub, then yanked on a pair of jeans and a denim shirt although he hadn't yet buttoned it when Mia appeared from the guestroom.

Her hair was damp and lay in soft tendrils around her face. She'd pulled on a thick terry cloth robe and looked clean and fresh and . . . relaxed.

Until he looked into her eyes. The old fear was there, haunting her, the night's events weighing on her.

"You don't deserve this," he said softly.

"Maybe I do for being swayed by Geoff in the first place."

"He hurt a lot of people," Alex said, forcing himself not to frighten her by touching her. "But I don't want you to think about him tonight."

She fiddled with her hair, then walked to the picture window overlooking his backyard. Woods, the creek, the natural beauty was so scenic it looked peaceful, like a postcard.

Of course, the woods were also the perfect place a predator could hide.

"Geoff doesn't know where you are, Mia." He walked up behind her, saw their reflections in the glass, recognized her wariness. And a hint of relief that she could take a break from the terror her ex-husband had instilled.

God, she looked so damn beautiful that his chest tightened, straining for a breath.

He couldn't resist. He lifted one hand and touched a strand of her hair, then brushed it back and closed his arms around her.

She sighed deeply and leaned against him, a heartfelt agonized sound, then turned in his arms and gazed up at him. Hunger, need, desire ... passion replaced the fear he'd seen earlier.

Unable to let the moment pass or resist, he lowered his head and closed his lips over hers.

CHAPTER 12

MIA CLUNG TO ALEX, savoring the sweet seductive allure of his mouth against hers.

She had been alone for so long.

Always terrified and looking over her shoulder. And just when she'd finally found peace, Geoff was back torturing her. Killing innocents to punish her for leaving him and testifying against him.

He would never stop hunting for her, never let her go.

"Don't think about him," Alex whispered in a hoarse voice against her ear.

"I can't help it," Mia murmured. "I want to forget about him, but he won't let me."

"I know it's hard, Mia." Alex kissed her again, slow and tender, achingly passionate. "But you're safe. I'm holding you, and nothing else matters right now."

A myriad of contradictory emotions pummeled her. Mia dug her fingers into his arms, willing herself to pull away for his safety. Willing him to hold her tighter and never release her. "I wish that were true."

"It is." Alex massaged the base of her neck with one hand. "For tonight, it's just you and me here alone." He claimed her lips again. "Just the two of us."

"I want that," Mia said softly. "I want that so much."

Alex cupped her face in his big hands. "Believe it, Mia. Trust me. I will never hurt you, and I won't let him hurt you either."

Mia's heart swelled with longing. The walls she'd built around herself to protect her heart crumbled.

Alex was everything she'd ever wanted in a man. He was promising her protection. And so much more...

A night of loving and tenderness.

Something she hadn't had in a really long time.

Something she desperately craved.

Resistance melted like snow on a hot day, and she tilted her head up and kissed him with all the pent-up longing she'd kept restrained for the past year.

Alex groaned at her acquiescence, tunneling his hands through her hair and drawing her closer. She sank into his arms, meeting his tongue with her own and inviting his inside to dance with hers.

Heat built between them as they deepened the kiss, and his fingers trailed down to pull at the tie to her robe.

"Tell me to stop and I will," he murmured against her neck.

She shook her head and raked her hands down his back. "I don't want you to stop."

"God, Mia." His breath bathed her neck, hot and heady, his need so potently strong in his voice that something inside her snapped, and she tore off his shirt.

His broad chest rippled with muscles so well defined that she had to touch them. Had to feel his hot skin, his muscles bunching as he drew a breath.

He dropped kisses along her ear and neck, his tongue flicking out and awakening the sensitive nerve endings along her throat. Releasing a breathy sigh, his head dipped lower to tease at the opening of her robe, and one hand parted the fabric.

Mia had never been shy or self-conscious until Geoff's critical scrutiny. Because of him, she had scars, inside and out. The instinctive need to hide them rose within her, and she pulled at the robe.

"Don't, I want to see you," he whispered against the curve of her breasts. "Remember, it's just me and you, Mia. Trust me. I want this." He kissed her skin so tenderly that heat flooded her, and tears sprang to her eyes. "I want you."

Mia heaved a sigh filled with resignation, with need and desire. All rational thought fled, and she gave in to the hunger inside her. "I want you, too. Alex."

He lifted his head at her admission and looked into her eyes. Need flared just before he lowered his head and kissed her again, this time so fiercely that she moaned his name.

A second later, they tore off each other's clothes. He tossed her robe to the floor, leaving her naked and vulnerable and starving for more of his touch.

She pulled at his jeans, the zipper rasping in the night as she pushed them down his hips. He kicked them off, stepping out of them, then she reached for his boxers.

He pressed his hand over hers, slowing her, but she wanted none of that. She wanted him naked and on top of her, inside her, all over her, loving her all through the night.

———————

PASSION AND RAW DESIRE overwhelmed Alex as he stripped Mia. He had never seen anything more beautiful in his life than the sight of her naked and hot for him.

But tonight wasn't about him. It was about loving Mia.

Showing her how gentle and loving a man could be. Especially a man who loved her

He froze, heart hammering out of his chest. Love? Was he in love with Mia?

Or was this simply an attraction? His need to protect an innocent woman?

Except Mia wasn't just any innocent woman. She was a woman he liked and admired. A woman he'd wanted but thought he shouldn't have.

Couldn't have.

And now here they were, kissing, stroking and tasting each other, and he never wanted it to stop.

She moaned his name again as he dipped his head and tugged one nipple into his mouth. He pulled her closer, then backed her toward his bedroom and eased her onto his bed.

For a moment, he paused. Breathless. So, in awe, he couldn't speak.

A drop of perspiration beaded on his lip. He didn't deserve her.

But he didn't have the willpower to walk away. Not when she opened her arms and invited him on top of her. Her lips seared his, her hands stroked his back then his buttocks, and his muscles clenched as he struggled for control.

Tenderly he trailed his tongue down her throat again to her cleavage and cupped both breasts in his palms, massaging one with his hand while he used his lips and tongue on the other. Eventually, he traded, loving each breast and suckling her until her body quivered.

Heat washed over him in a tidal wave of need, and he kissed her belly then parted her thighs and drove his mouth over her sweet center. She moaned again, her hips rising as she tried to draw him up to her, but he wanted to taste her essence.

Wanted her to know how much he desired her, that he derived his pleasure from pleasing her.

So, he flicked his tongue along her inner thighs, her slick wet folds then closed his lips over the heart of her sex and suckled her until her body began to tremble with her orgasm.

Still, he licked and sucked her, thrusting his tongue inside her as he wanted to do his cock, his body aching for release as she soared into sweet oblivion.

"Alex, please," she whispered. "I want you."

Smiling at her passion-glazed voice, he rose above her, braced his hands beside her head and teased her with his erection. She yanked his hips with her hands, then closed her hand around his stiff length and guided him to her.

He thrust into her, pausing for a second to let her adjust to his size, then almost lost it when she made a guttural sound and climaxed again.

The sound of her pleasure incited his own, and he thrust inside her, lifted her hips so he could drive deeper and began a rhythm that she met thrust for thrust. Sweat trickled down his back as the heat simmering inside him erupted into a blazing inferno, and he thrust faster and harder, deepening his penetration each time until he felt her inner core.

She clawed at his back, her breath panting as he rode her hard, reveling in the sound of her voice crying his name as the two of them came together in a blinding sea of sensations that sent him over the edge.

Even then as his orgasm claimed him, and he held her in his arms, he wanted her again.

One time would never be enough.

———

IN SPITE HER WORRY and exhaustion, Mia slept peacefully through the night.

Because she'd been well sated and loved for the first time in her life. Lying in Alex's arms was a miracle, she thought as she stirred and listened to the sound of his breathing.

But she couldn't get used to it.

When they caught Geoff, Alex would move onto another case—and maybe another woman. And she would have to pick up the pieces of her life and go on alone.

Alex opened his eyes and looked up at her, hunger flaring in the depths. Beard stubble grazed his jaw, his naked body powerful and even more sexy in the early morning light.

She wanted to stay in bed with him forever.

He reached up and stroked her cheek. "How do you feel this morning?"

Safe because I'm with you. "Good."

He arched a brow, and she smiled. "Well, I'm a little sore."

His smile faded. "From the attack?"

She shook her head, then climbed on top of him and straddled him. "No, from using muscles I haven't used in a while."

"Is that so?" His hands skated down her bare back as he lifted his head to tug one turgid nipple between his teeth. "Maybe another round will work out the kinks."

She threw her head back and laughed, but her laughter quickly turned to a moan as erotic sensations rippled through her. "God, Alex . . ."

His naughty chuckle echoed in the air, and he flipped her over, grabbed a condom from the nightstand, rolled it on and slid inside her. She closed her eyes and cupped his butt with her hands, a tidal wave of blinding colors washing over her.

He pounded himself inside her, thrusting hard and deep, over and over, and they rode the pleasure wave again until another orgasm built inside her. He whispered her name, nipping at her neck as euphoria carried her to its peak, then they came together, each moaning as their passion peaked and exploded.

For several blessed seconds, they lay curled together, basking in the aftermath of their lovemaking.

But Alex's phone trilled, interrupting the moment. Their gazes locked, and an apology filled his eyes.

"Go ahead and answer it," she said. She wanted this ordeal over with. Wanted Geoff back in prison where he belonged.

Alex eased away from her, and she felt oddly bereft. Not a

good sign. She was getting attached to him. Falling for him . . .

Geoff would destroy Alex if he knew.

Sobered by the thought, she rose from bed and rushed to the shower in the guest suite while he answered the phone.

"Sgt. Townsend," Alex said as he reluctantly watched Mia leave the bed. He wanted her back beside him, safe in his arms.

"It's Chief Dunn. You need to get over to the prison. Jones's cellmate says he'll talk but only to the original arresting officer."

Alex frowned. "All right, I'm on my way." He rose, quickly showered and dressed, then checked his weapon and went to the kitchen and brewed coffee.

By the time Mia emerged dressed, he'd made them an omelet.

"You cook?" Mia said, surprised.

He shrugged. "Not much. But I can do eggs."

She slid into the chair, although she looked wary like she was already distancing herself from him.

He didn't like it one damn bit.

"Mia—"

"Don't," she said, her coffee cup cradled in her hands. "Just tell me, what the phone call was about. Another murder?"

He shook his head. "No, my director wants me to talk to Geoff's cellmate at the prison. Maybe he has information about Jones's plans, where he's hiding out or going next."

Mia nodded and managed to eat a few bites, although she looked shaken, the earlier pleasure dissipating from her eyes.

She carried her dish to the sink, rinsed it and put it in the dishwasher. "Then let's go."

Alex stepped up behind her and rubbed her arms. "You don't need to go. I'm going to have a guard watch you while I'm gone."

Mia's shoulders straightened. "That's not necessary. I'll go to the hospital. I want to see Joy and Henry this morning."

Alex considered her suggestion. He could alert security guards. If she stayed with Henry and Joy until he returned, she'd be safe.

"All right. But you have to promise not to leave the hospital." Alex turned her around to face him. "Promise me, Mia?"

Her expression softened. "I promise, Alex. Just find Geoff and let's end this nightmare."

"I'm going to do my damnedest." He grabbed his own plate from the table and stacked it in the dishwasher.

Five minutes later, they were on their way to the hospital. When they arrived and parked, he walked her inside, then they rode the elevator to the second floor and Joy's room.

The older woman looked more rested and perky than she had the night before, although Henry looked rumpled and tired as if he hadn't slept for worrying about his wife.

He was so devoted to Joy that it touched something inside Alex. His own parents had divorced when he was small. His father died in a helicopter crash, his mother in a car accident a few months later. At six, he'd gone into the system in an endless sea of foster homes. None of them had worked out. He'd been bitter, angry and had shut down. One foster mother said he was hard to love . . .

The last home had scarred him forever. The old man had been abusive, had beaten the thirteen-year-old girl in the home until she'd bled to death. Alex had hated himself. If he'd been bigger, stronger, had shown more courage, he could have saved her.

Her death had haunted him and driven him to police work.

What would it be like to have a woman love him the way Joy loved Henry?

The way he loved Mia . . .

Mia rushed to Joy and hugged her, relief spilling across her features. "Joy, how are you feeling?"

"Like I'm ready to blow this joint," Joy said with a small laugh.

Alex pulled Henry into the hallway. "Are they releasing her today?"

Henry scratched his chin and headed down the hall to the vending machine to get coffee. "Doc said maybe early afternoon. They want to do an EKG first, just to make sure her heart's okay after the strain."

Alex explained that he needed to visit the prison. "Mia promised she'd stay here with you and Joy," he said. "Will you make sure she keeps that promise?"

Worry flickered in Henry's eyes. "I sure will."

Alex thanked him, then went to speak to the security guard. Once he informed the head of security about the threat to Mia, the guard agreed to watch Joy's room.

Relieved, Alex hurried down the elevator and out to his car. A half hour later, he was sitting in a visitor's room with Jones's cellmate Cyril Tyson.

"All right, Tyson," Alex said, his patience thin. "You wanted to talk to me?"

The beefy man gave a clipped nod. "I want a deal first."

Alex drummed his fingers on the table. "What kind of deal?"

"Move me to another facility and out of the general population."

Alex arched a brow. "Why would I do that?"

"Because I have information you want."

"Then spill it."

Tyson shook his head, the whites of his eyes bulging. "Not until you get me my deal."

Rage shot through Alex, and he leaned forward and hit the table with his fist. "I'm not playing games with you, Tyson. After you tell me what you know, we'll talk about a deal."

Tyson's handcuffs clanged as he folded his chunky arms across his chest. He seemed to be studying Alex, trying to decide whether to trust him.

"If you want out of the general population, that means you pissed off one of the gang members. That also means you're a dead man if you stay."

Tyson cursed. "Yeah, I did piss off somebody. But it wasn't a gang member."

Tension vibrated between them. "Then who was it?"

"Jones. That man's one crazy son of a bitch."

"Tell me something I don't know."

The man started to stand, and Alex tensed. The guard moved forward, hand on his weapon.

Tyson gestured for them to wait. "It's a piece of paper," he said. "The reason I asked to see you."

Alex exchanged a look with the guard, yet he remained alert

as Tyson slid his hand in his pocket. Just as he said though, he removed a scrap of paper that was folded into a small square. He dropped it onto the table and sank back into his chair.

Alex unfolded the paper, his stomach churning as he studied the vicious words and sketches Jones had made. Jones's version of the punishments he planned for Mia.

Lewd sex acts, the knife, the blood . . . Sadistic bastard.

"I know he's after his ex-wife," Alex said as if this drawing was old news. "Tell me something I don't know."

Tyson's black eyes bore holes into Alex. "He has funds set up in Brazil. That's where he plans to go once he gets his wife back."

Alex stared at him, waiting for more, but that was it. They'd suspected all along that Jones had made arrangements to skip the country. "Do you know what name he's going to use?"

Tyson nodded. "He has a passport and fake ID under the name Alex Townsend," Tyson said. "He plans to get away by posing as you."

"LISTEN TO ME, SON," Geoff's father told him. "The cops are everywhere. Maybe you should forget about Mia and leave the country now."

Geoff barely controlled his rage at his father's ridiculous suggestion. But he

had to because he needed his old man on his side.

Needed the money his parents had stashed for him so he could escape the country.

Then he and Mia could live the life he planned for them.

And she would never get away from him again.

"I will soon, Father," he said. "But I'm not leaving without Mia."

"She's not worth it," his father snapped. "The little bitch has already destroyed your life."

That was true, but there was no fucking way he'd let her go.

"I appreciate the concern, but everything's going to be fine," he said, injecting a calm into his voice that he didn't feel.

Hell, he should already have Mia by now.

Damn that Texas Ranger for interfering.

He would pay big time for that.

A siren sounded in the distance, and Geoff slid lower in the front seat of the pick-up. He had to keep moving. Stay under the police radar. "I have to go, Dad."

"When you get settled, we'll come for a visit," his father promised.

"Of course, but we'll need to allow sufficient time to pass for the police to stop watching you," Geoff said. Because they would hound his parents to death.

His father agreed and hung up. Geoff removed his new passport and studied it with a smile. Going away as Sgt. Townsend was a brilliant plan.

But first, he had to kill the real Ranger and get rid of his body.

Then no one would suspect that Geoff had assumed his identity. Yes, it was the perfect plan.

Sgt. Townsend's letter of resignation had already been typed. All he had to do was press send and everyone would simply think that he'd fallen in love with Mia and whisked her out of the country to keep her safe.

Then Geoff would never have to worry about the asshole again.

And he would have his wife back under his thumb as he should've had all along.

CHAPTER 13

MIA STRUGGLED TO TAME her nerves as she visited with Joy and Henry. Henry's phone buzzed, and he stepped out into the hallway to answer it. Joy had dozed off again, and Mia went to stand by the window.

A minute later, he came in, looking agitated. "That was Sheriff Leonard. Bo Coolidge called him and said he wanted to come in, that he had something to tell him."

"Bo, the trainer?"

Henry nodded. "I'm going to meet him at the sheriff's office. Will you stay with Joy till I return?'

"Of course, Henry. You know how sorry I am about all this."

"Just take care of my lady," Henry said in a sheepish voice. "I don't know what I'd do without her."

Mia didn't know what she was going to do without Alex when he left her either. And he would leave.

She was simply a job to him. Nothing more.

But she was terribly afraid she'd given him her heart and that it would be shattered when he walked away.

———————

ALEX PHONED HIS CHIEF the moment he left the prison. "Alert all the airports, train stations, bus stations and the border patrol that Geoff Jones is going to try to flee the country using my name."

"What?" Chief Dunn bellowed.

"That's the information Jones's cellmate gave me. Jones already has a passport and fake ID." The grisly drawings of the vile sex acts Jones wanted to perform with Mia haunted him.

"I'll get right on it," Chief Dunn said. "But he'd have to know that using your name would be risky and draw suspicion."

"I'm just relaying what Tyson told me." Alex paused. "Besides, if you think about it, it might work. He'll pretend to be me and say he's Mia's bodyguard. That he's taking her away for her own safety."

Chief Dunn made a clicking sound with his teeth. "All right, I'm on it."

They disconnected, and Alex strode to his SUV. His cell phone buzzed again, and he saw it was Sheriff Leonard, so he connected the call. "Sgt. Townsend."

"Sergeant, one of Henry's hands just came in and claims that Jones didn't kill Joleen Perry. He said that Truitt Wilson worked for another rancher before McCauley, a man by the name of Frank Sutter. Sutter thinks he owns half the county and has been trying to get McCauley to sell."

"He hired Wilson to kill Joleen to shake Henry up enough to sell?" Alex asked.

"No, Wilson claims he's innocent, but that after he talked to you, he started thinking about conversations he overheard at Sutton's ranch, ones that sounded suspicious. There's been a series of minor mishaps at the Crossties in the past few months, broken fences, cattle getting sick, equipment failure. I'm on my way to Sutter's to question him now."

"I'm leaving the prison now. I can meet you at his place."

"That's not necessary. My deputy and I can handle it."

"All right. Keep me posted." Alex passed through one guard's station, then made it to his car. He started the engine, then drove toward the guard's post at the far end of the parking lot. But when he approached, he didn't see the guard.

He slowed, the hair on the back of his neck prickling. Before he could climb out to check the station though, Geoff Jones stepped from the small building.

Alex reached for his Sig, but he was too late.

Jones must have gotten the guard's gun because he fired. Alex threw himself sideways in the seat to dodge the bullet, but it pierced his shoulder and pain ripped down his arm. He scrambled for his weapon and raised it to fire at Jones. But before he could retaliate, Jones jerked open the driver's door, aimed the gun at his leg and fired another shot.

Alex choked for a breath as pain suffused him. He swung his weapon up, but Jones knocked it from his hand with a karate chop. Blood poured from his shoulder and leg and the world started spinning.

Jesus, he was going to pass out. He had to fight.

But Jones slammed the butt of his gun into Alex's skull, and darkness engulfed Alex.

HENRY RETURNED AN HOUR later. Mia's nerves jangled as he explained about his talk with the sheriff.

Joy brushed her hair back with one hand. "I can't believe Frank Sutter would have someone killed just to get our property."

"He's a greedy man," Henry said. "I just hate that Joleen suffered because of that greed."

"Are you certain he had her murdered?" Mia asked. "Not my ex-husband?"

"It looks that way," Henry said. "Coolidge said Wilson had confided in him. We'll know more after the sheriff interrogates Wilson and Sutter."

Mia bit her lip. So, Geoff still could have killed the cook.

Either way, Joleen had been an innocent victim. Grief nearly overwhelmed her again. Joleen's death was so senseless.

Mia's cell phone buzzed. Anxious to speak to Alex, she stepped into the hallway and connected the call.

"Hello, Mia. I've missed you."

It wasn't Alex's voice on the other end of the line. It was Geoff's.

Mia's fingers tightened around the phone. "You have to stop this insanity," Mia said. "Turn yourself in before you get killed, Geoff." And before you hurt anyone else.

"You know I can't do that, Mia. I have grand plans for our future."

"You're a fugitive," Mia said tersely.

"Not for long." His tone went from flirty and taunting to menacing. "I'm your husband and you betrayed me."

"I'm not your wife anymore," Mia said. "The divorce was final months ago. I know you received the papers."

Of course, he had. That was probably what triggered him to plan an escape.

"Our vows said till death do us part, Mia. Have you forgotten?"

"They also said to love, honor and cherish. You didn't keep those promises, Geoff."

"Yes, I did, and you're going to keep yours."

"You can't make me love you, Geoff."

"No? Why not? Are you fucking that Texas Ranger? Do you love him?"

"That's none of your business."

"Actually, it is," he said darkly. "In fact, he and I are having a nice little visit."

Mia froze, her blood running cold. "What are you talking about? Are you with Alex?"

"Alex? Not Sgt. Townsend?"

Panic seized Mia. 'Where is he? Let me speak to him."

A sinister chuckle reverberated over the line. A low moan followed.

Alex?

"I'm afraid he's all tied up at the moment, Mia."

Mia closed her eyes, every muscle in her body tensing.

"What have you done to him?"

"He's losing blood fast," Geoff said in a low tone. "Do you want to save him?"

"Yes," Mia said, knowing she'd do anything to keep Alex alive. "Just tell me what you want."

"You know what I want, Mia."

"Yes, I do, you bastard." She sucked in a sharp breath. "Just release him and tell me where to meet you."

"Meet me, *then* I'll let him go," Geoff said.

Mia didn't trust Geoff for a second. He was setting up a trap and might kill them both. But she had to do something. She couldn't just stand by and let Alex die.

So, she struck a deal with the devil. She'd do anything to keep Alex alive.

ALEX SLOWLY ROUSED FROM the depths of hell to consciousness. His memory was foggy, but pain throbbed in his shoulder and leg.

He'd been shot. Twice.

By Geoff Jones. At the damn prison, the last place he'd have expected the man to be.

Where was the son of a bitch?

He blinked rapidly and tried to move but realized he was bound to a stake in some dark building, arms tied behind him, feet bound to the wooden post which held him hostage.

Sweat dripped down his hair and into his eyes, and he squinted, searching for the man who'd ambushed him.

But shadows plagued the corners, and the building was so dark he couldn't see a damn thing,

Was Jones hiding in the corner? Taking pleasure in watching him struggle to free himself while he bled to death?

Because the bullets hadn't struck any major arteries. They'd only pierced muscle, flesh and tissue, deep enough to cause a good deal of bleeding.

Enough that eventually the blood loss would kill him.

Was that Jones's plan—to make him suffer a long slow death?

Panic stole the air from his lungs. He didn't care if he died, but with him out of the way, Jones would probably get Mia. Did he have her now?

God, please no. He'd promised to protect her . . .

He couldn't allow his mind to go there. He had to think. Come up with a plan.

Figure out how to escape.

Because there was no way he'd let Jones kill the woman he loved.

Footsteps crunched. The smell of gasoline wafted toward him.

A board creaked, the hiss of a breath whispered through the air, and Alex knew he wasn't alone.

"You coward! Untie me and fight me like a real man," Alex said through clenched teeth.

Something hard slammed against his jaw, then another blow came. He spit out blood as Jones began to beat him until the world turned gray, then black and slipped away again.

———————

MIA DEBATED WHETHER TO ask the sheriff to go with her. She wasn't a fool. She knew she was walking into an ambush.

But before he'd hung up, Geoff had warned her she'd better come alone. That the moment he spotted a second person, he'd kill Alex.

She couldn't take the chance.

Besides, what did her life matter if Alex died because of her? She'd never be able to live with the guilt.

Because she loved him.

Dammit. She hadn't wanted to. She'd fought her attraction to the sexy Ranger and knew loving him was insane.

But her rational side had avoided the warning, and she'd fallen for him anyway.

Mentally reviewing tips from her self-defense class, she tugged on a jacket and stashed a canister of mace in her pocket. She tucked her revolver into her bra, then strapped a small switchblade to her ankle beneath her jeans.

Alex had dropped her off at the hospital, so she hotwired Henry's pick-up, then called and left him a voicemail telling him she'd borrowed it because of an emergency.

Somehow, someway she'd make all this up to him and Joy.

That is, if she survived.

Her heart roared in her chest as she sped down the old highway toward the deserted lodge where Geoff had told her to meet him. The place had been closed for two years for renovations, but the owner had filed for bankruptcy and the property hadn't been touched or visited in months.

A good place for a criminal to hide.

She just prayed Alex was still alive.

The pick-up chugged and churned over the ruts in the graveled road, gears grinding as she hit pothole after pothole and dirt spewed from the tires.

Woods surrounded her, the road narrowing through the thick foliage, an area known for hikers and hunters, and those who sought seclusion for days.

Tendrils of fear clawed at her insides as she slammed over a rough patch, and the truck vibrated so hard the impact jarred her teeth. But she clenched the steering wheel tighter, keeping the vehicle on the road as she barreled around a curve and skidded down a hill.

Ahead the foliage broke, and a sliver of moonlight streaked the battered rundown wooden building, which looked like it should be condemned.

She braked, slowing and steering around a pile of rocks and a pothole, then cut the lights on the truck and shoved it into park.

To the side of the lodge, tucked between a copse of trees, sat a black SUV. Alex's SUV.

The sound of the rusty pick-up screeching as she opened the door echoed in the silence. She automatically checked left and right, and the periphery of the house, her senses alert. Geoff was here. Waiting. Watching.

Ready to jump her any second.

She had to be ready. To fight.

She grabbed the flashlight from under Henry's seat, flipped it on, and slid from the driver's seat.

Her boots crunched gravel and twigs, an animal foraging in the woods nearby growled, then a noise sounded from behind her. She whirled around, her stomach lurching when she spotted Geoff aiming a gun at her head.

CHAPTER 14

Every muscle in Alex's body throbbed from the beating Jones had given him. Prison had obviously enhanced his physical skills.

He blinked, the world a blur as he searched the darkness for the creep. But he didn't see or hear him in the room.

He had to find a way to escape.

He struggled against the ropes binding his wrists. Pain ripped up his arms as he jerked and twisted, but the damn rope was so tight, he couldn't pull his hands through. Heaving a breath, he turned one hand to the side, using his fingers to work at the knot.

But a noise sounded from a few feet away, a faint stream of light seeping in, cloudy with dust motes, then he heard Mia's voice.

"Where is he, Geoff?" Mia asked.

"Keep walking, sweetheart," Geoff said in a menacing tone.

Footsteps echoed across the wood floor, the sound of Alex's own breathing punctuating the air. He strained for control, working more vigorously to free his hands.

"Alex," Mia called.

The door slammed shut, blocking out the light. Alex swallowed hard, trying to orient himself, but one of his eyes was swollen shut, the other blurry.

"Get out of here, Mia," Alex shouted. "It's a trap."

Suddenly the sound of a match being lit struck the air, then Alex looked up to see Jones holding the flame in front of him with one hand. His other held a gun to Mia's head.

Terror for Mia filled him. "Let her go, Jones."

Jones's sinister laugh reverberated off the walls. "Why, because you want her?"

"I want her to be safe," Alex growled. "Safe from you."

Alex gave Mia a pleading look, praying she'd understand and run. But her gaze rested on his face with a weary kind of resignation and fear blended with some other emotion he couldn't quite define.

He jerked his head toward Jones who looked wild-eyed and crazed with bloodlust. "Do whatever you want with me, but don't hurt her."

Jones answered with a cynical smile while tears filled Mia's eyes. She spun toward her ex-husband and touched his arm.

"I did what you asked, Geoff. I'm here. Now leave him alone and let's leave."

Geoff shook his head, his lips twisting into a snarl while Alex continued working the rope. He had one end through and was tugging it through the loop.

"If I leave him, he'll just come after us. Besides," he said with a victorious smile. "I need his name for us to escape. There can only be one Sergeant Alex Townsend."

A heartbeat passed. "You can kill me, but you won't get away with it," Alex said. Hopefully, the authorities had already been alerted to Jones's plan.

"Geoff, please. He's tied up, and no one knows where we are or that he's here." Mia tugged at Geoff's arm. "We can be out of the country before anyone realizes the truth."

"Shut up, Mia," Geoff said. "He's going to die, and it's your fault. You have to be taught a lesson."

"Like you tried to teach her when you beat her half to death," Alex muttered.

"She needs to learn to be an obedient wife," Geoff said as if his logic made perfect sense. He jerked Mia by his side, then tossed the match onto the floor.

It had been too dark to see earlier, but now Alex noticed that the man had crumpled newspaper around him in a circle. The fire caught the papers, fire crackling as it quickly spread around him.

"Geoff, no!" Mia reached inside her pocket, and Alex saw her pull out a canister of mace. But she wasn't fast enough, and Geoff karate chopped her wrist and sent the mace flying across the room.

Mia cried out in pain, and dropped to the floor, doubling over as if she was hurting. Then Alex saw her slip one hand beneath the hem of her jeans. Slowly she worked her fingers until a small pocketknife appeared in her hand. She folded her fingers around it to keep it hidden from Jones's view. Alex held his breath, praying the man didn't see what she was doing.

Geoff gripped Mia's arm to haul her back up, and desperation hit Alex in the gut. He struggled vigorously with the rope. But Mia quickly brought the knife down and jabbed it into Jones's leg.

Geoff bellowed in pain and reached for the knife, but she yanked it from his leg then ran toward Alex. She jumped over the flames and managed to slice one of the ropes around his wrist before Jones vaulted toward her.

Geoff was on her in a flash. He yanked her by her hair, dragged her through the flames, then slapped her across the face and threw her to the floor. His fist flew up next, and he slammed it into her jaw.

Alex cursed, hating the man with every fiber of his being. The flames were inching toward him, eating up the paper and licking at the pants of his jeans.

Mia covered her face to fend off another blow, and fire seared his ankle, catching onto the threads of his jeans as he desperately yanked at the rope to free himself.

Mia had taken beatings before. But this would damn well be her last.

Using moves her self-defense instructor had taught her, she brought both feet up and kicked Geoff in the stomach. He grunted, his expression shocked for a second just before rage seethed in his eyes.

"You bitch, you will learn," he hissed.

He dove at her, and Mia rolled to the side, lurching to her feet. But he tackled her, sending her face down. She caught herself on her hands and knees, but he was too strong, sent a blow to her lower back that made her collapse.

Blinding pain mingled with tears and nausea. Jesus, he knew how to hit.

But he was not going to win this time.

The sound of the fire crackling mingled with her own moan as she struggled for a breath. A second later, Geoff jumped on top of her, holding her down as he shoved her hair away from her cheek and licked the side of her face.

"You want me to show this fucker how a man takes a woman," he growled near her ear. "Then he'll remember that you're my wife, not some whore for him to touch."

"Geoff, please," Mia begged. Her cheek throbbed like the devil.

If she could get him off of her, maybe she could reach the gun she'd tucked inside her bra.

His laughter rumbled with evil. "Please what?"

"Please don't do this here. Let me up, and we'll go someplace nice and quiet. Then we can make real love before we leave the country."

She heard Alex fidgeting with the ropes as Geoff rolled her over to face him. God help her. Blood had soaked Alex's chest and pants. He needed a doctor fast.

If the fire didn't engulf him first.

She had to save them.

Geoff's gaze met hers, a heady sense of hunger blazing in his eyes as he traced a finger over her breast. "Do you know how many nights I dreamed about having you again while I was in that hellhole?"

She shifted, fighting nausea at his touch. "I'm sorry, Geoff. But you're here now, and so am I." She gestured toward the fire. Smoke was billowing around them, clogging the air and making it harder for her to see Alex.

He had to be weak from blood loss. And now he was inhaling smoke.

She faked a smile, forcing a soft flirty tone to her voice that sickened her. But she'd do whatever was necessary to save Alex.

"Let's get out of here before this old place goes up in flames."

Geoff studied her for a moment as if weighing her words for sincerity, then pushed off of her, stood and took her hand to help her up. Suddenly Alex tore loose and lunged at Geoff, throwing him sideways and sending them both crashing to the floor.

The two men traded blow for blow, but Geoff delivered a hard kick to Alex's wounded knee, and Alex groaned and fell backward.

Rage at Geoff surged through Mia, and she yanked the .22 from her bra, braced it in her hands and aimed to shoot.

"Get off of him," Mia hissed.

But Geoff wasn't listening. He jerked Alex up by the collar and ground his foot into Alex's injured leg. More blood seeped from the wound, and Alex's face contorted in pain, but he shoved a fist into Geoff's abdomen. The blow was hard enough to force Geoff to stagger back.

Her heart raced as she yanked the .22 from her bra, aimed it at Geoff's chest and fired. The bullet slammed into him, his eyes widening at the impact. Then he lunged toward her with a sadistic scream.

He knocked her down, but she pressed the trigger and released another shot.

Geoff knocked the gun upward though and the bullet hit the ceiling. Then he ripped the gun from her hand and tossed it across the floor. A second later, he wrapped his hands around her neck.

She struggled, kicking and trying to fight him off. But his fingers dug deeper into her throat. She was choking, suffocating, couldn't breathe.

She tried to fight, but he was so heavy, she couldn't move.

Dear God. After all this, he was going to kill her.

<hr>

ALEX STAGGERED TO HIS feet, disoriented from the pain. But Mia was fighting for her life, and he didn't intend to lose her.

Not now.

Smoke clogged the air, the fire spreading to the far wall and eating at the floor. The stake where he'd been tied was completely engulfed in flames.

Dammit. He was too weak to beat Geoff. He needed a weapon and had no idea what Jones had done with Alex's Sig.

Frantic, he visually searched the room and spotted Mia's .22 near the flames. He pivoted and spotted the shiny metal of Jones's .45 against the wall.

Shoving one hand over his chest to stem the blood flow, he staggered to the corner, bent over and picked up the gun.

Mia was gasping for a breath, kicking her feet to try to knock Jones off of her.

Cold fury engulfed Alex, and his adrenaline kicked in. He crossed the room in seconds and stood behind Jones, then pointed the gun at the back of Jones's back.

"Get off of her now."

Alex jammed the barrel into his back. "I said to let her go."

Slowly, Jones released Mia's neck. She gasped for a breath, and Jones raised his hands in surrender. But Alex didn't trust the son of a bitch.

And with good cause.

Jones whirled on him to get the gun. Alex didn't hesitate.

He fired the weapon, catching Jones straight in the heart. Shock widened the man's eyes as he realized he'd been hit.

Then he lunged at Alex.

Alex smiled, grateful he did. It gave him a good reason to shoot him again.

The bullet pierced Jones's heart, then he staggered back. Mia rolled to the side just before the son of a bitch hit the floor.

Alex stared at the man for a minute, then knelt and felt for a pulse.

Nothing.

Relieved, he stumbled forward, collapsed beside Mia and pulled her into his arms.

"Are you okay?" he whispered.

She clung to him, her breathing ragged. "Alex . . ."

"He's dead."

"We have to get out of here," Mia cried. "The fire's spreading."

"Go," he said. "I'll be right behind you."

She framed his face with her hands. "No way I'm leaving without you."

"Mia . . ." He was fading, the world spinning again.

"Come on, cowboy." She slid her arm beneath his shoulder and helped him to stand.

Together they wove through the smoke-filled room and through the door to the fresh air waiting outside.

Alex felt his legs buckling and tried to hang on. But he lost the battle and went down.

The last thing he remembered before he blacked out was Mia kissing him on the lips.

He wondered if it was the last kiss they'd ever share.

CHAPTER 15

Terror for Alex gripped Mia as she waited on the ambulance and sheriff to arrive.

His face was stark white, his breathing shallow. And he'd lost so much blood . . .

Fear mushroomed inside her. Would he make it?

The lodge was completely ablaze as the rescue workers arrived. The sheriff climbed from his car, his face earnest as he visually scanned the scene.

Mia waved the medics over to where Alex lay on the ground, hundreds of feet from the burning building, and they began to work on him, taking vitals, examining his injuries, using blood stoppers to help stem the flow of blood.

They moved him onto a stretcher, then started an IV.

"Is he going to be okay?" Mia asked, her heart in her throat.

The medics exchanged concerned looks. "It's hard to say,

Ma'am," one of the medics said. "He'll need surgery. We'll take him to the closest trauma unit."

The other medic narrowed his eyes at her. "It looks like you need medical attention yourself."

"No, I'm okay," Mia said. A few bruises were nothing compared to what she'd endured before. "Just get Sgt. Townsend to the hospital ASAP."

Mia wanted to go with him, but the sheriff was waiting on an explanation, so she told the medics she'd meet them at the hospital.

"What the hell happened here?" Sheriff Leonard asked as the ambulance raced away.

Mia explained about Geoff's call, that he'd ambushed Alex and shot him, then about the fight that had ensued inside.

The sheriff jerked his thumb toward the inferno that used to be the lodge. Rotting wood burned fast. "You mean Jones is in there?"

Mia nodded, her throat thick with emotions and raw from where Geoff had tried to strangle her. "Somehow Geoff got Alex. He shot him, brought him here and tied him up then called me. I . . . had to come, to save Alex."

The sheriff grunted. "You should have called me, brought back-up."

"I know," Mia said. "But he said if he saw any police, he'd kill Alex." Her voice broke. "I couldn't let him do that."

"And let me guess. When you got here, he tried to kill you."

Mia sighed. "I think he planned to kill Alex then take me away. But I fought him and shot him once with my .22. Then Alex got untied and they fought. Alex managed to get Geoff's gun and shot him with it."

"How did the fire start?" the sheriff asked.

Mia's anger churned. "Geoff. He tied Alex to a stake and was going to burn him alive."

"Jesus Christ," Sheriff Leonard muttered.

A fire truck wailed down the dirt drive, then the men jumped out, unrolling hoses and dousing the flames. The building was lost, but if the blaze spread to the woods, they might have more serious problems on their hands.

"I'd like to go to the hospital and check on Alex," Mia said. And she needed to return Henry's truck and apologize for borrowing it without permission.

The sheriff nodded. "I'll need a formal statement. But I'll catch up with you later."

Mia nodded, then jogged toward the pick-up truck, jumped in and sped away. The image of Alex's ashen complexion and his still body flashed in her mind, and she prayed that he'd survive.

SOMETIME LATER, ALEX ROUSED from consciousness. His body felt heavy, weighted, his leg and chest throbbed, and machines beeped around him. An oxygen tube was attached to his nose, an IV in his arm pumping God knew what into his system, and his chest was bare except for the bandages.

Memories assaulted him, and he managed to pry his eyes open and look around the room. Mia sat beside the bed wringing her hands.

Her face was streaked with tears, bruises marred her beautiful face, and her hand trembled as she reached up and squeezed his hand.

"They removed the bullets. The doctor said you were lucky."

Her words hung in the air, heavy with guilt and other emotions.

"Thank you for saving my life, Alex."

Alex's throat was so damn dry he had to swallow twice to make his voice work. "Are you okay?"

"Yes, now that I know you're going to make it." Mia released his hand and stood. "It was touch and go for a little while."

Alex grimaced. "I wouldn't leave you, Mia." He meant that in more ways than one.

Her eyes flickered with emotions, hope fluttering there for a second as if she read his meaning, but she didn't comment, making his gut tighten. What was going on in that mind of hers?

"The sheriff said one of Henry's neighbors Frank Sutter paid a man named Kurt Jeeters to cause trouble at the ranch to get Henry to sell. Joleen heard Jeeters talking on the phone to Sutter. That's why he killed her."

"I'm glad the sheriff caught him." Images of Jones's hands on Mia, strangling her, pelted him, and he reached for her hand again.

He never wanted to let her go.

But she fidgeted and backed toward the door. "I'll let you rest now. Thank you again, Alex. I'm . . . sorry for all the trouble I caused."

"Mia," he said, irritated by the distance he saw in her eyes. She was shutting down. Running.

Leaving him.

He knew it his bones.

She raised a trembling hand and gave him a small wave, then walked out the door without another word.

Dammit to hell. He wanted to go after her. But he tried to move, and machines beeped wildly like an alarm. He yanked at the IV, but two nurses raced in, giving him angry scowls.

"What do you think you're doing?" the heavyset one bellowed.

"Don't tell me you're trying to get out of that bed? You just had major surgery," The skinny one's voice was even more shrill than the first nurse's.

"You don't understand," he said. "I have to leave."

The heavy one pushed him back down. "You're not going anywhere, Mister."

"Nope," the other one said with a wag of her finger. "Not till the doctor says you can."

Alex cursed silently and glared at them. They didn't understand. He didn't give a shit how he felt or if he opened up his stitches.

Mia had left. And he was afraid he'd lost her for good.

Two days later, Mia stared at the ruins of the McCauley farmhouse, guilt overwhelming her. Joleen had been killed because someone had wanted to keep her quiet—the man who'd wanted Henry's ranch.

But he hadn't started the fire. Geoff's men had done that to lure her out as they'd originally suspected.

Because of her, too many people had been hurt. Henry. Joy.

And Alex . . .

God, she'd been terrified when she'd seen him tied to that stake, bloody, battered, and about to be lit on fire because she'd dared to leave her husband.

She knew what she had to do. Move far away.

After all, how could she stay and look into the eyes of all the people she'd caused so much pain?

Better for her to start over somewhere else. Geoff was dead, so she should be safe without assuming a new name.

She sat down and wrote Joy and Henry a long heartfelt note, telling them how much she loved them and appreciated all they'd done for her. She promised to send them payments to help rebuild their house as soon as she got a new job. Thankfully Henry had a small insurance policy, but it wouldn't be enough to replace everything. They'd need money for new furniture, curtains, and decorations. Joy had actually said she was excited about fixing up the place.

But Mia knew they were only trying to make her feel better.

She loved them even more for that.

She folded the letter and slid it into an envelope to drop off on her way out of town. Heart heavy, she retrieved her suitcase from the closet and began to pack her clothes and the few personal items she'd accumulated.

No family photos for her.

Except a picture of Henry and Joy. She carefully wrapped it in one of her sweaters and tucked it into her bag.

She didn't have a photo of Alex, but she would never forget his handsome face.

And how pale he'd looked on his deathbed.

Her heart fluttered with longing, but she tossed the rest of her clothes in the suitcase and zipped it up. Her boots went into a duffel bag, then she grabbed her jean jacket.

Sighing, she turned around and studied the cabin, memorizing the details of the woodwork, the horse paintings on the wall, the quilted throw Joy had handmade and draped across the foot of her bed.

This was the first place she'd felt truly at home as if she had a family. Sadness welled inside her. She would always remember it with love.

Suddenly a knock sounded, and she froze. Probably Henry or Joy coming to check on her or ask her about the horses. She'd already taken care of them for today.

Running her hands through her hair, she stepped to the door to open it and was shocked to see Alex standing on the other side leaning on a crutch.

His face was still black and blue, his eye purple but not as swollen, the stitches in his forehead stark in the evening light.

She'd never seen a more handsome man.

But something was wrong.

"Where the hell have you been?" he asked, his tone furious.

Mia gaped at him in surprise. "What's wrong? Was Geoff really not dead?" Jesus Lord, please let him be dead.

"He's dead," Alex said. "You'll never have to worry about that bastard again."

Her breath rushed out. "Then what's wrong? Why aren't you still in the hospital?"

His lips thinned into a frown. "Because I had to see you."

"Alex, you need rest, the doctor said—"

"I don't give a damn what the doctor said," Alex muttered. "I thought you'd visit me. And I called and left you messages, but you didn't return my calls."

He pushed past her, his crutch clacking on the wood floor as he scanned the room. His eyes fell on her suitcase, anger flashing.

"Are you taking a trip?" he asked gruffly.

Mia shifted nervously. "I'm leaving. Henry and Joy have suffered enough on account of me."

"Did they ask you to leave?"

"Well, no . . ."

He turned to face her, a muscle ticking in his jaw. "Do you think they want you to go?"

She bit her lip. "It doesn't matter. My mind is made up. I've hurt them too much already."

"You didn't hurt them, Mia. *Geoff* did. And Joleen died because of Henry's neighbor." He took a step toward her. "You are not responsible."

Then why did she feel so horrible?

Alex limped a few more steps, stopping only a hairbreadth from her. "But if you run off and leave the McCauleys, you will hurt them, Mia."

"Alex—"

"They love you, Mia. They think of you as family. Can't you accept that? When you love someone, you don't want them to be a martyr."

Mia took a step backward. Alex was invading her space. She couldn't be this close to him and not touch him. "That's not what I'm doing."

"Then you're running on guilt, *unreasonable* guilt."

"Maybe I am," she said, her defenses rising. "But every time I look at Joy, I remember her sprawled on the floor, hurt, her house burning around her."

"Those images will fade, Mia. Just give it time."

She shook her head, her pulse pounding. "No, they won't, just like I won't stop seeing you lying on the ground bleeding to death. All because of me."

He gripped her arms. "Not because of you, because a madman was after you."

"You were just doing your job," Mia said. "And I appreciate it, but you don't owe me anything else."

Anger hardened his chiseled face. "No, I don't owe you. I'm here because I want to be." His voice turned husky. "The McCauleys aren't the only ones who love you."

His husky words made her heart flutter.

Like a magnet, her gaze was drawn to his mouth. She wanted to kiss him. Tell him the truth. That she loved him so much that she was terrified of losing him.

But she couldn't make her voice work.

She didn't have to.

Alex tossed the crutch aside, then yanked her to him. "I love you, Mia. I love you and want you to be my wife."

Mia swayed. Had she heard him correctly? "But Alex . . ." He didn't know what he was saying. She didn't know how to be what he needed.

"Tell me the truth," he said, his expression braced for a fight.

"Do you love me?" he asked softly.

Emotions threatened to overcome her. A sob caught in her

throat. Her lungs strained for air.

"Mia?" He arched one brow, his black eye looking pathetic and painful, but his voice was low and sultry.

So seductive she couldn't resist.

"Yes," she whispered. "I love you. But I'm no good for you."

"I'll decide that." He yanked her against the vie of his thighs and nuzzled her neck with his lips. "Now say it again."

Titillating sensations enflamed her. "I love you, Alex."

He teased her lips with his tongue. "And you'll marry me?"

Her heart squeezed as his dark gaze met hers.

"Yes, Alex," she said, a smile tickling her mouth as his hand began to unbutton her shirt. "I'll marry you."

He brushed his lips against her cheek. "Then make love to me."

She shook her head. "Alex, you're injured—"

His sexy laugh rumbled against her neck. "Yes, I am, but you are just what the doctor ordered." He kissed her neck and walked her backward toward the bed. "Besides, you know us Texas Rangers. We like to live dangerously."

He stole her breath with another mind-boggling kiss, one filled with such tenderness and longing and hunger that Mia could no longer deny herself.

She seared him with a passionate kiss that left them both frantic to be closer.

Then together they undressed and made long, slow passionate love well into the night.

Other Books

If you liked *Safe in His Arms*, then please write a review on Amazon! You can also contact Rita at www.ritaherron.com and follow her on Facebook and Twitter @ritaherron!

The Manhunt Series
Safe by His Side (Book 2)
Safe with Him (Book 3)

The Keepers Series
Pretty Little Killers (Book 1)
Good Little Girls (Book 2)
Little White Lies (Prequel to Dead Little Darlings)
Dead Little Darlings (Book 3)

The Graveyard Falls Series
All the Beautiful Brides (Book 1)
All the Pretty Faces (Book 2)
All the Dead Girls (Book 3)

The Slaughter Creek Series
Before She Dies (Prequel)
Dying to Tell (Book 1)
Her Dying Breath (Book 2)
Worth Dying For (Book 3)
Dying for Love (Book 4)

THE DEMONBORN SERIES
Heartless (Book 1)
Mindless (Book 2)
Soulless (Book 3)

RITA'S LIGHTER SIDE
Marry Me, Maddie
Sleepless in Savannah
Love Me, Lucy
Husband Hunting 101
Here Comes the Bride
There Goes the Groom
Single and Searching
Under the Covers

ABOUT THE AUTHOR

USA Today AND AWARD-WINNING author Rita Herron fell in love with books at the ripe age of eight when she read her first Trixie Belden mystery. But she didn't think real people grew up to be writers, so she became a teacher instead. Now she writes so she doesn't have to get a real job!

With over ninety books to her credit, she's penned romantic suspense, romantic comedy, and YA stories, but she especially loves writing dark romantic suspense tales set in southern small towns.

For more on Rita and her titles, visit her at www.ritaherron. com. You can also follow her on Facebook and Twitter @ ritaherron.